# Tales of Arcadia

By the Same Author

*Novels*
Summer Sure to Die
The Marriage of Raphael Kerr

*The Hampshire Romances*
Edmund Persuader
Tomazina's Folly

*A Novella*
Elissa Wyatt

# TALES
## OF
# ARCADIA

Stuart Shotwell

MERMAID PRESS OF MAINE

Copyright © 2024 by Stuart Shotwell. All rights reserved.

The moral rights of the author have been asserted.

All rights reserved. No part of this publication may be reproduced, stored in a retrieval system, or transmitted, in any form or by any means except by permission of the author.

With the exception of the three essays contained here, this book is is a work of fiction. Names, characters, places, and incidents either are the froth of the author's imagination or are used fictitiously. Any resemblance to actual persons, living or dead, or to locales or to current or recent businesses and events is entirely coincidental.

This is a reprint, with corrections, of the 2000 edition, with a new afterword and the addition of a previously unpublished story.

Publication Data
Shotwell, Stuart (1953–).
Tales of Arcadia/Stuart Shotwell
p. cm.
ISBN 978-0-9841032-0-1 (alk. paper) 1. NewEngland—History—
19th century—Fiction. I. Shotwell, Stuart (1953–). II. Title.

Conceived, written, edited, designed, typeset, and produced by Stuart Shotwell.

Cover images: Leon Kroll (1884–1974), *Morning on the Cape,* ca. 1935. The original work is oil on canvas, 36 × 58 in. (91.4 × 147.3 cm). Carnegie Museum of Art, Patrons Art Fund, 36.1. Photo credit: Carnegie Museum of Art/Art Resource, N.Y. The front cover image is a detail of the painting shown in full on the back cover.

This book is distributed directly from the publisher at www.stuartshotwell.com. Mermaid Press of Maine regrets that it is not able to acknowledge, consider, or return manuscripts submitted in any form.

The chearful sage, when solemn dictates fail,
Conceals the moral counsel in a tale.

—Johnson

# Contents

# Preface

To this purpose we design to set up a new Arcadia.
—Cervantes

In this Age of Iron it has become necessary to explain what Arcadia is.

Arcadia is no place. It is in the mind of the poet or the writer who retreats to it. As Vergil showed us, it is by no means an ideal world. It mirrors the strains of the writer's life and times.

My Arcadia is perhaps more georgic than others. It is part Maine, part wider New England, part old England, part the classical Arcadia. During a time of great and sudden personal growth it became the place from which I could speak most freely. If I had tried to set these stories in the concrete world, they would never have come into being.

Most of these tales deal with an old theme, the struggle for understanding of oneself in the context of companionship. As a result, familiar situations can be found in them: acts of love, temptings, separations. Through many of these situations I have passed; and yet I have not strictly depicted my own life in any story but in those that form the introduction and the conclusion.

In short, I caution my friends that although it is possible to make fiction from facts, it is not possible to make facts from fiction.

# Saul's Road

The Cranberry Harbor Road is now no more than a track. I walked down it for the first time not long ago, imagining what it was like in the last century. There were a few farms along its route then; a housewife might have come to the door and listened when she first heard the distant rumble of a wagon on its ruts. She would know from the sound whose wagon it was, wave briefly or not as it lurched past, and be back at her chores before the last creaking echo faded among the firs.

The farms are gone, of course. The only ruts I saw in the crusty March snow had been cut by some joyrider's all-terrain vehicle. Actually, there were others—the imprint of the runners of a wide sled, relentlessly parallel. Fitting, that a road that led down into the past—and I wish, into the future—was marked by human passage, both modern and outmoded.

The Cranberry Harbor Road once linked the north and south sides of the easternmost neck of Maine, where the state abuts on the Bay of Fundy. It was a shortcut between the saltwater farms clustered around the labyrinthine coves of Cobscook Bay to the north and the pastures, woodlots, and blueberry barrens on the Fundy shore. This part of Maine is mostly deep sand and gravel dropped by glaciers over volcanic rock; short, high ridges cross the land in bands that run from east to west, showing the lines at which the glaciers parked for a time in their advance or retreat. But the Cranberry Harbor Road runs against the ridge lines, taking to the low ground. Where I walked, alders crowded close on either side of the way, forming a thicket of ghostly gray stalks. They show the bog land, where water is trapped on the surface by compacted glacial clays. To the Yankee mind, the alders are anathema, as they creep out of the swales into the fields—the first sign of neglect, of nature reasserting itself over land once cultivated. A less human-centered view holds that they are the first healers of the land—that they fix nitrogen in soil exhausted by human use.

This bog was hardly the *selva obscura* of Dante, but in my progress it would have to do. I emerged from it suddenly into a barren. The road went straight on across the open country; the sled tracks turned, and I followed them, suspecting they went where I meant to go. Up a bank, over the broad uneven curve of rough field rising upward toward the sky, treading the stiff crust of snow that was just beginning to yield to the thawing sun, I wended over the rolling land for a minute or two before I saw the house and a figure in the window. "Saul!" I called, then louder, cupping my mittened hands. He looked up and waved slightly.

On my left was a dormant garden and two large compost piles, built foursquare with logs in the Scott Nearing style. On my right was Saul's view: a small heath, a ridge clad with birch, fir, and spruce, and, more distantly, the Porcupine, a granite hill that with its sloping spine and bristling conifers looked very much like its namesake, as if crouching and lifting an armor of quills before backing into an enemy. (There are four hills called the Porcupine on this eastern peninsula. That rounded shape was a favorite of the sculpting glaciers.)

Saul's house—he calls it a shack—is about the size of the cabin Thoreau built by Walden Pond, although that is due to coincidence rather than conscious emulation. Saul put up the place himself. The handsplit cedar shakes that cover it seem a good inch thick. I was pleased to see the large windows: although simple and rough, the land here is too beautiful to leave outside.

So much for his shelter. The rest of his economy, in the root sense of the word, is as simply described: Saul grows his own food, makes his own clothing of handspun wool, and has but one cash product, the spoons and ladles he carves of apple and poplar and other native woods. These he occasionally peddles by pedal and by foot, selling them at prices that he feels reflect the value of his labor. He could easily make far more if he chaffered with rich collectors at craft fairs. But that would be against his principles.

And Saul operates from principles first. He came to this land on the Cranberry Harbor Road years ago not to drop out of life, but to plunge into it. At first he felt he had to teach the doctrine of Doing Without; he went around the community proselytizing, challenging others to live more simply. But with time he saw that his example was more powerful than his preaching. And his neighbors could hardly help but see that he was not the one who was doing without. They themselves, whose daily round led them from house to car to job and back again, whose hands touched nothing raw, nothing fresh, no unformed material needing realization, they were the true withouters. Besides, Saul denies any readiness with words. He would rather act. If you begin with your principles, he says, the way to your destination becomes clear. If you consider the destination first, anything can happen to your principles on the way to it.

He met me at the door. I stepped first into a small room with a board floor. A shaving horse stood to one side; various saws for cutting firewood hung between the round fir studs. Overhead were food-drying racks made of muslin stretched on rectangular frames.

I followed him into the main room, where he resumed his work over a large tub of steaming water. He had perched it on a three-legged stool over the hatch that led down to his root cellar; the rest of the floor was stone, the surface uneven. The stones were a recent and cautious innovation: for years he had had only a dirt floor. The walls in this room were covered, too: with books by Tolstoy and Gandhi, the thinkers he studies most; by jars of beans, seeds, and the wheat he mills for flour; by utensils for cooking, spinning, knit-ting, sharpening, grinding, and preserving. On a shelf were two baskets woven of cedar bark, on a bench a skein of gray yarn wound on a niddy noddy. I sat on a stool by a desk on which stood an open bottle of ink and several homemade pens; I looked around at the walls, the cookstove, the view through old glass, and I watched him work.

He was washing wool, he explained; the moths had laid eggs in his supply. He described with humor how they had suddenly hatched—"moths everywhere"—as he went on wringing the mottled fleeces with careful vigor. The vigor is a hallmark of his, although he is certainly unaware of it. He eats nothing but healthy food, his entire life is an act of exercise; his movements display the unhurried and yet deliberate concentration of a man without a boss looming over his shoulder or a clock on the wall counting off the minutes until freedom at five.

We talked for a while of various matters. I suppose I mostly listened at first, but finally I told him why I had come.

I was at a crossroads. Circumstances were offering me a choice: I could buy out my wife's equity in our house and land (she was going her separate way) and take on an even greater mortgage debt; or I could put the place on the market, sell out, and start over more simply elsewhere, paying my way as I went, and avoiding the crushing cost of money.

The property in question is a homesteader's dream: fifty acres, four in fields and the rest in mixed tree growth; two ponds; apple trees that even without culture nearly groan with fruit each fall; and a house, solid if unfinished. I loved the place, although I was determined to move on, if I had to, without regret.

I came to visit Saul not for his advice, but to see for myself the way he lived. For too long I had had Thoreau's redundant litany on my mind: "Simplify, simplify, simplify." I did not need a push toward simplifying as much as I wanted to see an example, to gauge in what degree to proceed. But Saul had a suggestion, and made it unoffensively. "Build your own place," he said. "Anyone can build all the shelter they really need. A little land will do; you don't need a lot."

But he wanted to know the principle at work. "Why do you want to do it?" he asked.

"I love to write. I've written about a dozen novels. Some are terrible. Some are publishable, or at least I think so, but I can't get them published. I'm not really that interested in seeing them published, except insofar as it would help me write more. I don't want my enjoyment of what I love most to depend upon the say-so of an editor in New York. In three months I can make enough by writing nonfiction to live for six, if I live simply."

He thought; we talked some more. Finally he came back to his own principle. "It seems to me," he said, "that people have to see where the common good lies, and live as best they can to serve it. The way I live may not overwhelm the world, but it's a work I do for peace and for the health of the Earth and society. What troubles me about what you're suggesting is that I don't see in it any way you'll be serving others."

"Well," I said, "I think of Helen Nearing. She loves music; when she went with Scott Nearing to Vermont to find a simpler life, that was one of her goals, to enjoy her music. I think as an artist, she had to look inward first, to be true to herself first; and the rest, the service to the world, came both afterward and with her affirmation of her artistic self. Both the Nearings are great examples of how to live sanely; and I think they started by finding themselves in a simple way of life. In that way what I do can lead to a benefit for others. And I haven't let go of the hope that someday what I write will be of some larger effect, although I don't want to build my life on that expectation."

Saul nodded. "We each have to find our own Light," he said. "And that is the first step. Once we've found it, we can work for others within it."

We talked still more—of Tolstoy, of felting wool, of house building, of the land again. He offered me mint tea sweetened with honey. Then he remembered that he wanted to try his two-man saw with me, to show me, he said, how fast the work went. In years past he had proposed sharing the task of cutting firewood, but my life had always been too crowded with other responsibilities. Now the prospect did not seem so hopelessly busy.

We took the saw and went outside; in a minute a log from his woodpile was on the buck. The saw cut with almost fiendish rapidity, almost no effort. I had often used a two-man saw that had belonged to my grandfather, but it had never been as sharp as Saul's. Now we tried another log; it jumped about on the sawbuck as we worked, and after we had cut it we discussed ways one might use to hold the logs fast. I enthusiastically advocated an invention of my own, a contraption of chain that clamped the log to the buck. Saul was interested, but was not sure the answer had to be so complicated.

"Well," I said, "genius is in the refinement."

"Yes," he said. "But you don't have to be a genius to solve problems. That's one of the things I learned when I came here. I didn't know how to do anything, but I learned how from other people, or I figured it out." He laughed, an exclamation of humor and humility that made gentle what he said next: "I think not having to do things makes people stupid."

Although he invited me to stay for lunch, I had work waiting at home. "Come back some time," he said, "and we'll do something. Talking is all right for a while, but I find that if I talk too much, it makes for a bad night's sleep."

We exchanged goodbyes. I went back up the Cranberry Harbor Road through the wood and the bogs toward the world.

Although Saul had accepted my explanations, I wondered as I walked if he had not done so more out of generosity than persuasion. Was I not really looking at the goal first—that I find time to write—rather than at my principles? The question I should be asking was not *how* I was going to write, but *why* I was writing. My feet slowed in their mechanical progress.

I had been writing for thirty years and yet I had never asked that question. It was always an end in itself, the writing. I had even wasted time—years—in writing that was not my best, because I found themes or plots addictive in themselves. I had confined myself often to books that could never have become more than second-rate. They were too easy to write; they were the writer's version of the cheap thrill. "Read the good books first," said Emerson, "or you may not have a chance to read them at all." The same is true of writing books. You have to write your best books first, or you may use up your life writing the easy ones.

I came to a stop. To the west of the road at this point lay Saul's woodlot. I knew it was his because the tree stumps bore marks of an axe rather than a chain saw. The wood looked almost like a park; a mind had been at work, selecting and making use of resources rationally. I thought of a tree on my own land that had been taken over by a porcupine—a handsome fir rendered as bare as a utility pole, its bark in musty tatters at its base. That was the way I had gone about my writing, as blindly as a porcupine gorging itself on bittersweet bark.

I began to walk again.

By not taking on the constant moral challenges of life, it seemed to me, by not confronting the meaning of our actions on the wider stage—we become morally "stupid," just as those who never have to cope with practical problems become too "stupid" to solve them. We squander energy, resources, time, perhaps with a nagging sense that we would like to live differently, but in reality somewhat stupefied by the meaning of the choices we are making.

And there is, I believe, a knowledge within us that can make those choices intelligible. We have to see what our basic principles are and work from them. If we want peace, we cannot make war. If we want a clean Earth, we have to stop staining it with poisons. If we want a simple life, we have to say no to complexity. And if we want to live a life that enables us to create, we have to understand the larger purpose of our creating.

At length I came out of the dark wood and stood in the sunlight. I knew I had more thinking to do; but it seemed I had at last found the right question to ask myself.

I know that everyone does not live on Saul's road. I probably will not live as simply as he does. But I am sure that his principle is right: If we know who we are and feel worthy in ourselves, we make the choices that are for the good of all.

# Hands

For J.L.W.

They ran away from the picnic together. Robban's sister saw them go, and observing the sacred duty of all younger siblings, reported the deed at once to her parents. There were smiles and mild laughter; and sure enough, Robban's lank figure and Perenna's plump one could just be seen, disappearing out of sight where the wood grew up at the head of the gorge. They were already holding hands.

Robban's mother turned to Perenna's. "You don't think they're too young, do you, to be off by themselves?"

Perenna's mother laughed. "I was just going to ask you if you didn't think they were too old."

"Fourteen is an in-between age," said someone.

They ran through the wood laughing at their escape. Cool, green shadows—silent steps on the crumbling humus—a jay protesting.

Robban was six feet tall. His dark shock of hair seemed to be falling continually forward into his eyes. His bones seemed of drawn wire.

Perenna had not yet grown out of all her childish roundness. Her cheeks were cream and rose, clear and soft. In just the right light, whenever Robban was holding her close, he could see an almost invisible golden down on her face.

At the pool they found a hollow beneath a ledge of rock where they could sit on soft moss; a screen of spicy-smelling fern hid them from the path to the fields, but gave them a view on the waterfall. She sat within the brace of his arm and leaned her head upon his hard shoulder.

Then they sat still, without speaking, needing nothing, knowing nothing but right now. From time to time she turned up her face and they kissed, just enough to keep the sleepy blood stirring, to make them dizzy and glad.

In her two hands she held his free hand. It seemed to her like a thing living in its own right. It moved continually within hers, caressing and responding.

The afternoon passed away without their noticing. Towards its end she spoke.

"Do you know what this is like?" she said, in an awed whisper.

"What?"

"Like being in church," she said. "See, where the light shines down on the waterfall like the sun streaming through a big church window? And the waterfall is so high, like a church tower; it's like God's blessings pouring down on us. And the pool is like God's love, where you can ease your thirst, and the water is always sweet, and never runs out."

"If we were in church, I couldn't kiss you," he said.

"No, but we could hold hands. Just last meeting day I saw old Avery and Rebecca holding hands. I think that would be the most beautiful thing on earth—don't you? To live your life with someone you love, and sit in church when you're old and hold hands."

She was wiser than he was. He did not understand what she meant. He knew the sense of her words; but he thought love was more worldly, more active, more outward; and though he said nothing, in secret he doubted.

"Sing me something," he said, after a time. She demurred, but he insisted.

"All right," she said. She let go of him and moved away, on her knees, to the front of the hollow. Turned toward the waterfall, she folded her hands before her, as if she were indeed in a church, and raised her round face to the light shining on the foam and the rainbow mist below.

She sang a hymn. Her young voice was beautiful. She loved to sing; as she became an instrument her cheeks glowed, her lips moved in a smile, and her eyes saw into another place.

Robban's father, coming to call the children back for the ride home, heard the clean, sweet tones of her song, and reproached himself for ever worrying what they might be doing.

The man sat alone at the end of the dock. The lake was broad from east to west, and he faced west, where the sun was sinking, making the water into white fire that stung the eyes. He had had a boy bring out the chair for him; he often sat out here, looking over the lake that had made him rich. Sometimes he would spot one of his own schooners making upwind, loaded with lumber, apples, cheeses, or with finer goods like balsam resins, woolens, or linens.

On this afternoon, however, the lake was calm, and its stillness increased as the day waned, until it became as quiet as the pond among the Stetton hills where he had his big sawmill. From time to time his gaze followed black ducks or loons winging with amazing speed across the surface, mere specks almost consumed in the blaze of reflected sun.

Hooked into the back of the chair was a long cane. His right leg, stretched before him, had been broken in an accident when he was twenty-five, and had not healed straight. He had walked with a limp for forty years.

His stride was not all that was crippled. As he heard a babble of children's voices on the shore, he turned about suspiciously, lowering his head and staring beneath eyebrows that he now knit together in vexation over the bridge of his nose, as if even from this distance he could frighten others into silence.

An older woman had come down to the shore with her grandchildren: three girls and two boys. With sweet, shrill, and affectionate voices they called to her, teased her, chattered about the lake. He guessed they were from the village, she from away. He turned his back to them again, debating whether he should inform her that she was trespassing on his land.

"The lake is so still," she said. "Hush, children, listen to the lake for a minute."

Peace stole back over the waters. Then, unable to resist, the children tested the echoes with ear-piercing shrieks. He gritted his teeth and darted the group a hostile look that went unnoticed.

"Hush," the woman said again. "Chloe, why don't you sing for us?"

The other children added their encouragement. Chloe seemed to be a favorite.

He was on the point of rising and sending them away; his shoulders were tensed, his hands clenched. But then Chloe's song began. He remembered it at once; remembered how it had lit the spaces of the gorge, ringing clear above the muffled ruffling of the falls plunging into the pool.

He remembered Perenna; the intensity, the closeness, the simple union of two. He saw himself again, a lanky adolescent with his hair in his eyes, and her with her round cheeks, the lashes that fringed her eyes, half-closed as they kissed.

A very physical pain went through him, the symptom of a psychic ill. There was something wrong with his eyes—he could not see the lake. He put his hand to his face and realized he was weeping.

He had not wept for nearly fifty years.

As the child sang on, a sob broke from him. He tried to choke it back, but another followed. He could only weather his emotion, the way a ship weathers a storm. He put hands on his knees and bent his head, letting pain for things lost surge out of him.

The song ceased. Childish applause, and a warm grandmotherly commendation. Robban sat for several minutes, recovering, drying his face with his handkerchief. He wanted to be kind to these children. He might have some sweets in the warehouse; perhaps the woman would accept a scarf, or he could have a wheel of his best mountain cheddar sent up to her.

When he thought he had removed the marks of his emotion, he took up his cane and hobbled back to the end of the dock. The grandmother was now seated on a pile of timber, refereeing a game of tag. At first Robban did not look much at her; instead he picked out Chloe. She was a pleasant-looking child, nothing out of the ordinary; and yet when he compared her looks to the hard, sensual beauty of his own daughters, he had hopes that her heart was better and that her life would be happier and kinder than theirs. He turned his attention to the grandmother, and limped closer.

She looked up at him. For a moment they each saw only a stranger; but then with a start they recognized the children within the aging flesh.

"Perenna!" he said. She stood up, amazed.

"Robban?"

He was afraid the sobs would break loose again, but they did not. Some tears did, though, as she came forward, with shining eyes, and seized his free hand in two of hers.

"I always knew we would meet again," she said.

"You were faithful, weren't you?" he said huskily. "And I was not."

"It was a great match for you," she said, smiling generously. "Besides, we had been apart five years by then. Five years is a long time when you're young."

*And not so long when you're old,* he thought. Right now even fifty years did not seem long to him.

"And she was rich, and beautiful. And she brought her family to the business, which I never could have. Everyone knows how well you did."

"No, Perenna. I did poorly. My wife was always unhappy. She was a low woman, no matter about her family. And my children went bad, every one of them. I made my money, but I would have done better without it. It's done nothing for me."

She was genuinely grieved for him. "Sit down here," she said. "Let's talk for a while."

He hobbled over and sat stiffly on the timbers. She moved as lightly and easily as she had fifty years ago.

He asked her about herself. She told him she had been married twice and twice widowed. Her husbands seemed to have been good solid men, the type he would have once dismissed as dull drudges. Now he thought they might well have been better than he. In any case, they must surely have been happy with this cheerful, generous partner. She was now living two towns over; her daughter and grandchildren had just moved to the village by the lake, and this was her first visit.

He told her more of his own life; he was ashamed of it. He had spent too much time in bitterness.

Before he was half-finished the children were eager for her attention. She sent them ahead and then turned to Robban. "Why don't you come up to see me at home sometime?" she asked. "I'm leaving here Wednesday. Any time after that will be fine."

"Don't ask me if you don't mean it," he warned her. "I'll take you at your word."

"I hope you will," she said, smiling at his reserve.

"Then I'll be there. Shall I send word I'm coming?"

"Just come."

She stood, and he rose too, leaning on his cane. "I'm glad," she said. "If I know you're coming to visit me, I won't have to hurt again now, saying goodbye."

"Yes," he said gloomily. "Remember what that was like?"

"You, walking behind the wagon," she recalled sadly. "And waving, waving until I could see you no more."

He went up to her town on the next Saturday. A man by name of Clark worked for him in the village there, and Robban had sent orders to the fellow to make ready to lodge and feed him. It meant enduring a supper with Clark and his wife. Clark puffed and hemmed pompously, and seconded Robban's every remark; his wife fairly cowered in terror through the whole meal, afraid to jeopardize her husband's position by revealing her stupidity with some thoughtless comment. When he asked them what they knew of Perenna, however, the woman suddenly became effusive. Robban left the table silently vowing that Clark should have his place for life.

He went over early the next morning. To his surprise he met Perenna coming out her gate. "Bound away so early?" he asked in disappointment. She laughed gently at him.

"Do you know what day it is, Robban?"

"Of course. It's . . . Sunday."

He realized now that she would be going to church.

"How long has it been since you went to meeting?" she asked him.

"A long time," he said. "I never go."

"Well, then, come with me."

She closed the gate and put her arm through his. He had to walk slowly because of his limp; but her pace fell in readily with his.

He realized now that the busyness he had noticed in the little village was due to preparations for the meeting.

On all sides gates were clicking shut and families were bustling down the road. Farmers from the outlying lots drove rumbling wagons crowded with fresh-faced children; their placid wives waved happily as they saw Perenna, and eyed the tall, sharp-faced man beside her with curiosity.

"Tell me the truth," Perenna said as they walked. "When was the last time you went to church?"

"The day I was married," he said.

She shook her head in wonder.

"By the next Sunday I was too angry at God to go," he explained. "I had been so sure I was doing the right thing—that I was following God's will for me; and I found out so soon that I was wrong. I said to God, If it was your will that I marry this woman, you have to save me from this awful marriage. I couldn't save myself; I didn't have the will to do it. For forty years I didn't have the will; and then my wife died. It seems to me now that we were never really married at all."

"Sometimes when troubles come," she said, "prayer is the first thing that goes. We forget how to listen to God; we blame God for our own failings."

"If that was a test of me," he said, "I wasn't ready for it. There wasn't enough strength in me to be tested."

She put her other hand on his arm.

As they neared the meeting house he had a sense of tributary streams joining; from near and far people gathered, passed through the great doors, and found places in the crowded pews. Perenna led Robban to her accustomed seat. A gaggle of country girls made extra room on the bench, their solemn eyes peeking out at Robban under the edges of their bonnets.

"Do you still sing?" he asked Perenna as they sat down.

"In church I leave that for younger voices. But I'll never stop singing, not until the day I die."

The meeting began. Robban had expected to feel irritated—at what, he did not know, perhaps some hypocrisy he imagined he would find. He expected to feel an outsider, a lone sinner sitting among the worshipful. Instead he felt taken in with the people about him, accepted and made one with them. The words that he heard made unexpected sense to him; the prayers and the invocations of God awoke an old belief that his bitter years had not extinguished.

The choir began a hymn. It was not the one Perenna had sung that day, but another he remembered from his childhood. As the young voices rose through the sunlit spaces of the church, Robban thought again of the waterfall and the brimming pool.

*There is a God,* he thought. *There is a God that pours Its love into this place, because here people are ready to receive it. If I were willing to receive it, I could find that love here too. I could find it wherever I was.*

He looked at Perenna. Her cheeks were still round, her eyes still bright. The music still gave her a view away into another place.

She saw that he was looking at her and she smiled at him. Suddenly he held out his hands, both of them. She was surprised.

Then she remembered, and took his hands in hers.

# Necessities

Bion had not always been a severe man. But he prided himself on being a practical man; and his practical side led him into severity little by little, without his noticing it.

He had a fine house where he lived alone with a housekeeper. One day when no one was in it, it burned down. "Good riddance to it," one of his neighbors heard him say, as he surveyed the smoking ruins; "I didn't need so big a house." He built himself a smaller one; indeed, it was hardly more than a hut. He gave the housekeeper a good sum and sent her away. There was no need for a housekeeper without a house, he said.

One spring as he was planting it occurred to him that the herbs that seasoned his broth were really not necessary. What was flavor? He did not need it. A potato was a potato, wheat was wheat. So he grew no more herbs, and ate his food ungarnished. As for the wheat, why bake it into bread, only to grind it up with the teeth and turn it into mush instantly? Why the foolishness with rising and kneading? He would eat flour and water, and it would do his body as much good.

Books, too, he eschewed. The Book was enough, he used to say. More than enough, he would have joked, but joking, too, was superfluous. He gave away or burned the other books he had.

In this way he simplified his life. His neighbors visited him in order to marvel at him, and to go away, worrying and puzzling over his abstemiousness; although he thought they secretly feared he might be right. Once he overheard a woman saying to her husband, "How does he do it?" And her husband answered: "He has a big barrel of philosophy, and he flavors his food out of that. A mighty big barrel of philosophy." And this piqued his pride. In time he saw little use even in his neighbors; and since use was his yardstick for all, he began to be very much alone.

His life was very narrow, but very controlled. He seemed to be pleased only when he found some way he could do without something he had. And in this way he lived for several years, giving up more and more, until he had really only one more thing to give up: life itself.

And though he had no intention of giving that up, it seemed he would have no choice in the matter. One summer he grew very sick. His joints ached; he had swellings and sore spots in his groin and his neck; he felt light-headed and weak. He lay in his hut on the blanket that served for his bed, looking out at the changing August sky, wondering what was wrong with him. He was sure only that it was not something new that he had eaten, or something unusual that had he done; for he had eaten nothing new and done nothing unusual in quite some time.

At last things grew very bad with him, and he began to slip away. Just at the moment he felt he was on the verge of death, hands lifted him; he was being carried, swaying and jerking, among familiar but unrecognizable men. The trees overhead went by indistinctly, and he heard birds singing their evensong; and even in the delirium of his sickness and his fast he wondered why they sang, of what use it was to them.

He came to himself again in a fine large room. Overhead were beams of oak, carven with sayings from the Book. Into the ceiling, with great cleverness, the carpenter had let a skylight, the only one Bion had ever seen. Through its wide square was a pure blue expanse, given depth by the passing masses of clouds. When he turned his head, he saw that nearly all of one wall, above the carved wainscotting, was made up of leaded windows, giving a view over an immaculate garden. Just outside the glass at one corner of the room a cluster of sunflowers raised their brilliant yellow heads. They bobbed slightly in the breezes, as if nodding to one another in encouragement.

When he saw the garden, he began to remember it, and after several minutes he realized that he was in the house of Carstook and Phoebe, his neighbors. He managed to roll his head about to look at the bed; it, too, was worked over with carvings and figures.

After several minutes Phoebe entered the room. She was tall, with a pleasant face, and the ample, well-rounded figure of a woman who has borne many children. They had all moved away now, and she and Carstook were past their strongest years; still, she was yet vigorous, as her garden attested.

Her words that day were hardly more than soothing chatter. She propped him up and got some gruel into him; he felt its strength almost at once, and could move about a bit on the bed, though his joints still ached.

He did not respond much to her questions and to her cheerful speech. It seemed unnecessary to do so.


Bion grew stronger slowly. Within a week he could sit up, even at times move about the room. Mostly, however, he lay propped on the bed, pondering the sunflowers, the garden, or the roofbeams, with growing irritation.

One day Phoebe came in as usual with his food. He complained that it was too rich. He needed no butter on his bread; he needed no bread. Why were there herbs in his soup? Why had she not brought him water instead of milk?

She listened to him with the indulgent smile parents save for a child fractious with fever. He saw he was making no impression on her, and at length gave up. "It's ironic," he said finally, "that I should have wound up in such a house."

"Ironic?" asked Phoebe. "What do you mean by that?"

"I mean that I have chosen to live my life without any useless ornament, and I have been brought to a place where every inch is covered with it. You've spoiled a good solid roofbeam with decorations and lettering. You've tainted your garden with idle flowers. This morning I heard you singing as you worked out there. What use is that? It's wasted breath. When you lean over me I can smell perfume; and you have rings on your fingers. Everywhere I look, listen, smell, taste, feel, I find impractical and unnecessary things."

When he was through this outburst Phoebe regarded him with wide eyes for a moment. Then she threw back her head and laughed, heartily and joyously.

"And your laughter—" he began to add testily.

"—Is unnecessary," she finished for him.

"Exactly."

"And you think, dear neighbor, that it's an accident that you, who have given up all ornament, were brought to be healed in the house of two people who delight in it?"

"An unfortunate accident."

She laughed again, although somewhat more sadly, and sat down on the edge of the bed.

"Look outside, Bion. What do you see, there, outside the windows?"

"I see sunflowers. Surely you can't tell me that you harvest the seed? It's hardly worth the work."

"No, I don't harvest the seed."

"Then what do you plant them for? Why do you weed and water them? There's no point in it."

"If you'll be patient, I'll tell you."

He sank back listlessly on the bed and listened as one who had no choice. She leaned forward and spoke fervently and eagerly, and yet with a kind smile on her face.

"I would plant those sunflowers, and weed and water them, if they had no seed to harvest at all. As it is, they have seed, and I let the birds take it, as my offering to them; for God has said that they will be fed and clothed, and if I give them seed, I further God's work in my own small way. But even if those sunflowers had no seed, I would grow them. Why? Have you ever noticed, Bion, how in the morning when the sun rises, those plants are turned toward the east? How in the noon they lift their faces toward the zenith? And how at sunset they are turned toward the west, worshiping the strength that gives them life? And when the flowers open and their heads are too heavy to move, they face east, even all through the night, waiting, sure the light will come. When I look at them, they teach me how I, too, should face toward God, morning, noon, and night, remembering the strength that God gives me. Can you tell me they have no use? They remind me to look joyfully toward God. Isn't that a noble use? What are we here for on Earth, except to learn the will and the work of God and to do it? And doesn't everything on Earth teach us what God is, in its own small way, if we have the will to learn from it? So it is with every flower in my garden, great and small.

"You've been fretting over the carvings in the beams, have you? One night Carstook and I stood in this very room, arguing over something—over something that didn't matter—we were tired, and hungry, and the children had been shouting, and it had been too long since we had been together by ourselves. And while I was saying some cruel thing to him, he rolled his eyes, and by chance looked up and saw those words up there." She pointed them out to him: SEEK PEACE AND PURSUE IT. "I say by chance, but it was no chance that they were there, because he put them there. And when he saw them he wept, and when I saw him weeping, I was ashamed, and I looked where he was looking, and I wept too. And we came back to love for each other again, we came back to God again. Is that useless ornament if it reminds us of God? And it needn't be a word; there have been times when the love Carstook put into the making of this very bed, into the carvings of it, steadied me when I looked upon it, cherishing who he is and what he has done with his life."

He would not speak, so she went on.

"You heard me singing this morning. What did you hear me singing?"

"A light tune it was. A love song. It wasn't any church hymn, that I know."

"No, it wasn't a church hymn. It was the song that my Carstook sang when he was courting me. How do you think it makes me feel, when I sing it and look back over the years, the good years with that man—they've been rich and full, but dear God, haven't they sped by! When I sing that song my heart is full of joy and sorrow at once. Isn't that knowing God? I love church music, but there isn't a hymn that can make my heart full like that old tune.

"Who are you, Bion, to set yourself up as judge over what has use in this world and what doesn't? God put us all here—man, woman, child, beast, tree, and plant—let God approve our use. I never in my life knew the use of a common fly, but I'm sure God does.

"Or maybe you've gone so far that you think God itself is unnecessary?" (And in truth, Bion had from time to time wondered this.) "Well, if you have, I pity you, and pray for you, but I can do nothing else. What do you think God is? God is the reason for life. That's all. Nothing more or less. If you live, then you believe in God. Some little part of you, somewhere, believes in the reason for living. You may not care for the God of the priests and the Book, but you care about the God that is life, no more, no less.

"No, Bion, it was no accident that you, a dying man who had given up all delight in God's ornamenting of this Earth, should be brought to the home of a woman and a man who revel in it. It was no accident that you were dying and we were living. There was a good reason for that."

He was scowling. "You think I made myself sick, then?"

"I do. Or God did, to teach you something."

He made no answer.

Later that same day Carstook came in to visit him. He did not sit down. He stood up, his great wide shoulders nearly touching the beams, his head hanging forward on his powerful neck as though he had knocked it on that oak before. Bion felt the vitality of him, in contrast to his own feebleness. The big man's eyes were kindly, though, gentle as Phoebe's.

"I hear you're persisting in your old ways," he said quietly.

"Don't misunderstand me, neighbor," said Bion. "Phoebe is a good woman. But I can't agree with her. She's just not logical, not practical."

"And are you logical? Are you practical?"

"Yes, I am."

"And you're bitter and unhappy and sick, and she's joyful and happy and well. Maybe she's more practical than you think."

This had a certain sting to it, and Bion reacted somewhat harshly. "But she's a woman," he said.

"She is, God bless her!" said Carstook with a laugh. "And I guess she's proved that to me many a time! She's the only one I could ever find who was as keen on loving as I was, and I guess that's why we had so many children." He scratched his neck and grinned a wry, fond grin. "Well," he said, "the children are gone now, but the loving hasn't stopped." He looked at Bion again, smiling. "But I suppose you think that's all unnecessary. Why is it you never married, Bion?"

"A wife is a just a pointless ornament," said Bion.

Carstook laughed, delighted at the absurdity he had just heard; his laugh was much like Phoebe's. "Oh, she's an ornament all right," he said. "When I come back to the house after a day's plowing, and she puts a hot meal in front of me, I do think, 'Just an ornament!' And when I get a cold, and she puts the hot towel on my chest to ease the cough, I do think, 'Just an ornament!' And when I sit by the fire on a winter's evening, and the storm's howling outside, and I look across at her, I do think, 'Just an ornament!' Aye, and when we lie abed, and I put my hand on her in the middle of the night, and she snuggles close to me, I do think, 'Just an ornament!' She's an ornament I couldn't live without, and I guess that makes her a necessity. What are we put on this Earth for, but to share one another's company? That's where we find God best, it seems to me, struggling through the hard parts, and dancing through the good parts, with our family and our friends. Love is a necessity, Bion, not an ornament."

To this Bion had nothing to answer; and in a minute more Carstook went away, still chuckling to himself and saying, "Just an ornament!" as if he could not wait to share the joke with Phoebe.

Bion grew better in spite of himself. After a month he went back to his hut. His neighbors had harvested his crops for him, and laid them up in storage; indeed, they had added many foods he had not had planted. Amarylle had baked bread for him, and Grove had left him a jug of fresh, cool milk hanging by a cord in the well. These things he ate without allowing himself to question their utility; for he had noticed, although he would not admit it to himself, that this varied food made him stronger.

By then it was late September and Indian Summer was coming on. He sat in the sun in front of his hut with little to do but think. He thought of Phoebe's sunflowers. He thought of Phoebe and Carstook both; of Carstook's big hands carving those leaves and flowers and frills and letters in the oak.

He had been home about a week when he heard the bell tolling down in the village. He started, curious at first; but then old habit persuaded him that it was unnecessary to concern himself for the dead.

By and by he went down that way anyway. He had been walking about a little, and he thought the exercise would do him good. The service was long since over, and the mourners had left; he drifted through the churchyard, thinking he might find a clue as to who had died.

Thus he came on Phoebe. She was sitting by herself on a stone bench beside a freshly filled grave.

He sank to the ground beside her. He could not speak, but she could; she even smiled softly at him.

"My man has gone on," she said.

Bion nodded mutely.

She bent her head, eyeing him as gently as ever. "You know what I've been sitting here thinking?"

He shook his head, still wordless.

"I've been thinking what a blessing he was to me, all my days," she said. "Or maybe you think he was just an ornament? Oh, Bion, what is all this talk of ornaments and necessities, anyway? There are no ornaments, there are no necessities; there are only blessings."

Bion could not find the words to tell her that at last he understood. Nor could he find any words to console her, which now he found he very much wished to do.

Instead he groped about on the greensward and felt a clump of the last wildflowers of summer growing along the foot of the bench.

And these he plucked and held out to her.

# Thyme

I

Lysbet was in the thyme. The bees sang about her, as busy as she was, visiting even the stalks she had cut and cast down on the broad, checkered cloth; it was as if they hurried to cull the last sweetness from the blossoms, as if they knew that in another minute their mistress would tie up the four corners, swing the fragrant burden on her back, and go up to the house.

She, too, was humming to herself. Sometimes she was happy; this was one of those times.

The thyme bed was dug along the fence; the fence lay along the road; and along the road at this particular moment came a wagon groaning under a load of timbers. She noticed it, and straightened up to nod to the driver. Being neighborly was her determined policy; she told herself that if she was always friendly, someday she would win out against the slander.

The sun shone full on her face even under her bonnet. She felt suddenly curious, and shaded her eyes to see who was coming. She did not recognize him. He must be a newcomer, or someone from another village.

The wagon slowed as it neared her; then, as though on an impulse, hesitantly at first, the driver reined in, and sat staring at Lysbet as if in wonder.

For a very long time, perhaps a minute, neither the woman nor the man spoke or moved. It seemed necessary to invent a pretext for their interest in one another.

The man coughed weakly. "Would you have a cool drink?" he asked. The fine dust on his face and clothing and on the freight in his wagon, on the wagon itself and the backs and necks and foreheads of the sweating horses, made his request plausible.

Lysbet turned away and went to the well, which was distant about two hundred feet, and came back with a dripping bucket and a dipper. She climbed the fence before he could protest, and stood beside the wagon.

She could not understand the look on his face. It was almost a kind of fear. She did not stop to think what his eyes saw: a woman nearing thirty, light-boned and high-breasted, graceful, silent, with thick dark hair spilling out even from the ample bonnet—and the measureless golden eyes. He smelled the thyme her hands had gathered and her boots had crushed. And as he drank the cool water, sweet as corn in the field, his spirit drank in a like refreshment from the sight of her.

"Who's your husband?" he blurted out, rather stupidly, and immediately crimsoned under the yellow road dust. She smiled wryly.

"I don't have one," she said. "Who's your wife?"

He laughed. Lysbet liked his laugh.

"I'm not married either," he said.

She crossed her arms and raised one eyebrow slightly. "Why not?"

He laughed again, more easily. "That's what all my neighbors want to know. Haven't found the right woman yet, I guess. What's your excuse?"

"The same."

She smiled at him. He stretched on the wagon seat and had another drink.

"Where do you live?" she asked. "You're not from around here."

"Dunham. You know Farmer Moschus?"

"Up the mountain road? Yes, I know him."

"He has a little woodlot up in Dunham by me. Oak, mostly. He cut some timbers up there for his new barn." He nodded at the load. "Raising's tomorrow. His boy came up this morning, said his wagon was broken."

"Oh." She took back the bucket and the dipper as he held them out. They looked at one another as they had before.

"Going to the raising?" he asked.

"I expect to," she said, although in truth she had not till that instant made up her mind.

He grinned as though the heat were getting to his brain. "Maybe I'll see you there," he said.

He clucked to his horses and started off. She stepped back and watched him go. "Thank you for the water," he added, over his shoulder.

As the wagon went across the side of the hill and away, her thoughts went away too. Dreams, dreams, years of dreams seemed to burst inside her as a wild rose bush heavy with buds bursts into blossom, only instantly and all at once, so that she saw all the colors of her hopes, smelt them, felt their silken petals, heard future pleasure humming as it fed upon their sweetness, swallowed hard longing for their taste.

*I like him,* she told herself. *If only he doesn't—if only he doesn't believe what he hears. What did I say to him*

*when he asked me why I wasn't married? 'The same.' I
should have said more.*

She was not sure, when she became aware again,
how long she had stood there. The sun seemed different. The dust had settled again all along the road.
She turned about, confusedly, trying to remember what
she had been doing before he came.

Kristin was standing by the fence, watching her.
She, too, looked almost frightened. "Are you all right,
Mistress?"

"Yes," said Lysbet vaguely. Then, more assertively:
"Of course I am. I'm fine."

"Why are you standing in the road with the bucket?"

"Someone wanted a drink."

Kristin's gaze stole wonderingly along the road and
back to Lysbet.

"You silly thing!" said Lysbet. "Do you think I'm
dreaming it?"

"Well, where is he now?"

"He's on his way to Farmer Moschus's barn raising."

"But that's not till tomorrow."

"That's right. And I'm going."

"Am I?"

Lysbet was starting to climb over the fence, but now
she halted.

"No," she said. "No, I think you'd better stay here."

She avoided Kristin's eyes as she stepped down into
the thyme. Neither of them could speak for a minute,
though their pain spoke.

"Who is he?" Kristin asked. Her voice was hard and
hopeless.

"I don't know. He seems nice." She gathered up the
thyme in the cloth.

"Is he married?" asked Kristin.

"No."

"How do you know?"

"He told me so."

"Just like that? He told you so?"

"Just like that. Help me with this thyme, will you?"

"You've gathered too much, Mistress. Whatever will we do with it all?"

"You can never have too much thyme," said Lysbet. But they both knew she was just saying the first words that came to her.

2

She did not expect to see much of him at the raising. She was with the women, and he was with the men. But she quickly found out his name. The women had been only barely civil to her until she had asked for that information point-blank. Their minds had been full of cold suspicions and uncertainties; they wanted to snub her, but many of them had children her herbs had saved from sickness, even from death, and they were torn between gratitude and revulsion. But when she had said, suddenly, seeing him on the team of men heaving up one of the huge bents of timber—"Who is that stranger from up Dunham way?"—then the women had warmed toward her, sensing new possibilities. "His name is Thursis," they said. Mrs. Moschus told her more, while the rest listened, nodding approvingly, wondering if they might be able to like Lysbet after all.

"He has a very good farm up there next to our lot. Over two thousand acres, they say. His hayfields go on over most of the front; and there's oak in his woodlot, same as ours. His barn is stone, and he's got good water, close to the house. He had a brother who had claim to the place, but he died two years ago. This Thursis just came back and took over about a year and a half ago; he was running a farm down country for someone else. He's good at it, too. Biggest ears of corn I ever saw, when we went up last harvest."

Betty Moschus paused and turned her big eyes on Lysbet, like a velvet-eyed cow looking for a milking. "The woman that marries him will have a good setup, I guess," she concluded.

The other women added more, rumors they had heard. They were good at passing on rumors, Lysbet knew. They warmed to the work. But not a one had much to say about what kind of man he was.

At dinner the men sat at the long tables and the women brought the food to them. Lysbet went about with a great basket full of thick slices of her own bread and served them liberally. The men were grateful while she was putting food before them, but when they looked up into her eyes and saw who she was, their manner grew cool and they turned away.

She went to his table last, and then only because an inner voice chided her: *How much longer are you going to wait to be happy?*

When she reached his place she gave him bread from her nearly empty basket. In all this time he had not noticed her, though he had been glancing about in a furtive way, between his jests with Moschus and the other men. As she put the bread on his plate he saw her with surprise and smiled broadly.

"I've been wondering where you were," he said.

"Here all along."

"And I didn't even get your name yesterday to ask after you."

"Lysbet."

He held out a strong hand. "Thursis," he said.

"I know."

He grinned. "You know already? What else have you heard about me?"

"Well, I guess I know your cash value to the penny."

He smiled still and said, "A bachelor is public property, you know."

She frowned, irritated at all roles, formalities, the petty impediments of courtship.

"Will you be here after?" he asked.

She nodded.

"We'll talk a little, then," he said.

She went away content.

After supper someone had a fiddle. Lysbet and Thursis watched the dancing for a while and then went and sat on the stone sill of the doorway of the new barn. They talked for a long time. Or he talked, at least; it was not until much later that she realized that she had said little of herself. He started out by telling her all over again what the women had already said. Most of it was true, except that the farm was only five hundred acres. She listened between his words, trying to hear not the value of the land but the value of the man; but she could not quite make it out.

It was not until he spoke of his parents and his brother, all dead now, that she felt she learned something of him. She liked what she learned: he still grieved for them all, even for the brother whose death meant his own wealth. He said he'd give the farm a thousand times over and more to have his brother back; he was fervent, and she believed him.

The moon rose and lit his face. His features were well-formed, clear, and honest. She was overwhelmed by the man-ness of him; she wanted to reach out and put her hand on his chest, to feel the muscle moving beneath the cloth of his shirt; she wanted to lean close to him and feel him pull her to him. She yearned so much that she thought he must surely notice; and after a time she heard little that he said, though she seemed to hang on every word. She felt she had already made up her mind, although she knew it was too soon.

A boy came looking for him. "We're going, Mister," he said. "Wagon's all hitched up. You coming with?"

He stood up. "I'll be along in a minute," he said. "You tell your pa to wait for me." The boy raced away.

She rose reluctantly. "You can't be going back to Dunham tonight?" she asked.

"No, I'm staying with some kinfolk of Moschus's. My horses are there."

"Well, then . . . you'd better go."

"Yes," he said.

But he did not move. She looked at him, but he kept his eyes on the ground. "I'll be going by your house tomorrow," he said.

"Why don't you stop in? See the place."

"I've heard you're kind of a witch with herbs," he said, laughing. He had spoken to someone about her, then, during the afternoon.

"You'll hear worse than that about me," she said. "But none of it's true. Remember, none of it's true."

He looked up curiously. And once he looked up, he could not resist; for if ever a woman wanted to be kissed, it was Lysbet then, waiting for her life to begin.

The moon cast a dreaming softness over his features, but his kiss was hard. When he had gone away, she put her fingers to her lips unconsciously, as if trying to feel the remnant of something male.

As she gathered her things, Betty Moschus sought her out. "What do you think?" she asked.

There was no point in pretence. "He seems like a good man," she said. "But it's hard to tell. He talked, but I felt as if I couldn't get to know him."

"That's the way men always are. I've been married thirty-three years, and I don't know my husband a bit better than when I married him. Sometimes I think it's because there's nothing to know. Nothing they'll tell you, at least.—No, don't worry about getting to know him. That'll come, if it's meant to. As long as he's not an outright bad one, and he's got a good place. That's the way a good marriage is made—on a good farm. And you'd bring your house and land to the marriage too. That's a nice little place. You could sell it and give Thursis some coin when he marries you."

The older woman paused, thinking it all through. Then she seemed to shudder. "What about . . . what about that Kristin girl? What would you do about her?"

Lysbet drew herself up. "Why?" she said coldly. "What should I do about her?"

And Betty Moschus hurried away without another word, her big eyes darting about, not like a cow now, but like a frightened deer.

When Lysbet came home she found Kristin still awake. She was surprised; Kristin had often sat up for her, over the years, but she had always fallen asleep in her chair. Kristin could fall asleep in a few minutes, anywhere, at any time; she was still like a child. Even though she was only four years younger than Lysbet, people thought of her as a girl, not a woman.

It was easier to come home to find her asleep. Then all the mute hurt would be sleeping, too, in the child-like face. Lysbet would put her hand on the blond head and wake her, shoo her off to bed; and Kristin would stumble away, forgetting the reason for her vigil in her joy that Lysbet was back.

But now the pain was awake, waiting and watching. Lysbet could not control or disarm it. "Good evening," she said as she came in. "Did you have a good day?"

"I finished tying the bundles of thyme," said Kristin.

"Did you put them in the attic?"

"Yes, Mistress."

"Good. We've had good drying weather." She bustled about, doing the last chores that kept her from bed.

"What is he like?" asked Kristin in a hollow voice.

Lysbet paused, considering whether she should be offended, but in the end she decided that it would hurt Kristin more if she feigned ignorance. "He seems nice," she said.

"That's what you said before."

"Well, he still seems nice. You'll see for yourself tomorrow. He's coming to visit."

"Where would you like me to go, Mistress?"

"Go? Nowhere. You'll stay right here and meet him." Kristin took a slow breath, of surprise, relief, hope. "Really?"

"Yes. Really. Why not?"

"I don't know—I thought—"

"Go to bed," said Lysbet. "Go to bed and go to sleep. You were foolish to sit up and wait for me."

Kristin went to the door of her room. It was on the first floor; it had once been a sitting room. She paused at the threshold and then turned about.

"Did you kiss him?" she asked.

Lysbet was suddenly very angry; but it was late, and she refused to yield to the emotion. "Go to bed," she said sternly. Kristin knew what her tone meant, and went into her room with a cringing, slinking step.

At dawn Lysbet woke up. The birds were beginning to stir and sing; and she felt that her hope, too, was beginning to stir and sing, after a grievous long time, her entire lifetime to this day. She listened for a while in a pleasant, warm, drowsy reverie, thinking of Thursis, even of the house with the well near the door.

Then a little sound caught her ear. She sat up in bed, turning onto her knees and seizing her pillow as if she meant to hurl it.

Kristin sat on a chair near the door, watching her. The trails made by her tears as they fell down her cheeks were just visible in the soft green grayness of the summer dawn. When she saw she was discovered she started guiltily.

"Get out!" cried Lysbet. "Get out! Get out! Haven't I told you? Don't ever, *ever,* come into my bedroom!"

And Kristin fled with a little sobbing cry, like a child who has been slapped by her mother.

3

"Now, don't worry," said Lysbet soothingly when they had finished tidying the house. "You don't have to say anything unless he asks you a question." She plucked at Kristin's dress unnecessarily, straightening imaginary wrinkles.

"Yes, Mistress."

"And he may joke with you about being a witch. So just smile, if you can't think of anything to say."

"Yes, Mistress. Are you sure you don't want me to be out of the house?"

"Quite sure. You're my oldest and best friend, and I want him to know you."

"Mistress?"

"I wish you could stop 'mistressing' me while he's here.—What?"

"If you . . . if you did . . . marry him, could I still . . ."

"Be my friend? Be my help in everything I do? Come live with me on his place? Of course you could. I've always told you that."

"What if he doesn't like me?"

"If he doesn't like you, he doesn't like me."

Kristin seemed to take some hope now; she saw a way out of the immediate danger that she would lose Lysbet forever; although in truth Lysbet had always assured her that she would not forsake her when she was married.

"Now," said Lysbet again, "I'm going to go out and watch. Look busy, whatever you do. Let's not let on that we did anything special because he was coming."

Kristin looked down at her best dress, which she did not particularly like to wear, and puzzled over the falsehood. It was part of her simpleness that she could not fathom the occasional necessity for a polite lie.

Lysbet strode out into the dooryard. The summer heat was already strong. Thursis would want to start early to beat the worst of it. Already she had to shade her eyes to see across the hillside. When she did so, she picked out the plume of dust raised by wagon wheels on a distant part of the track.

Her joy was strong in her. She meant to wait in the house, or at most somewhere in the dooryard; she had a vague idea that she should be doing something when he came, and look up nonchalantly; she would certainly frighten him off if she seemed too eager—he would think she only wanted his farm. The truth was that she would have taken him farm or no farm. But the closer he came, the more her feet led her away from the house, down toward the road. She had actually reached the gate by the time she could hear the wagon coming around the hill.

It was Thursis right enough. He seemed to be eager too, for he held the horses to a good pace, though it meant that he was bounced and jarred roughly on the seat of the empty wagon. She smiled, and smiled, and could do nothing to quell the smile: it rose out of her happiness; it rose out of her future; she had never had such a smile before, and she enjoyed it too well to disguise it with the frown of a coquette.

On he came. But he did not look at her. And he did not slow the wagon. As he approached the gate he gripped his hat and set it askew on his head so that its broad brim hid his face.

And the wagon rolled by without stopping.

She raised her hands; she called out. Had he mistaken the place? Was he playing a joke on her? She ran after the wagon; and here the horses stumbled on some loose round stones in the road and slackened their pace enough for her to catch up.

"Thursis! Thursis!" she called. For one last moment she had a hope that it was all a joke, as he kept his face averted from her; but then he turned, almost whirled about on the seat, and glared at her fiercely.

And she knew that he had heard the lies, and that he had believed them all.

She stopped running and let the wagon go; but something in her went after it, and in the place where that something had been came a lancing pain that made her hold her head and sob, instantly and wretchedly.

When she found her way back up to the house, Kristin was waiting inside, obediently churning butter. As she saw Lysbet she shrieked. "God! God!" she cried. "What happened?"

"He drove by," wept Lysbet. "He looked me right in the eye and drove by."

"Why? Why would he do such a thing?"

"Because he heard what they say! Why else? Last night he kissed me and today he hates me. Why else?"

Kristin wept even more desperately than Lysbet herself.

"It's all my fault!" she cried. "It's all because of me!"

"No," said Lysbet, "it's not you. It's their lies, their lies. I told him not to believe them, but he did.—Why? At every turn of my life, the lies have pulled me down, pulled me back—I can never go forward, never go on—I'm stuck here, with all this love I can give to no one!" She wept on, shaking and tottering.

Kristin groaned, as if at an old familiar grief. She came to Lysbet and held her, perhaps fearful she would actually fall. But Lysbet pushed her gently away.

"No," she said. "Don't touch me—I can't bear it. It just makes me think of the lies. What will I do? I can't just let him go away believing what he does—"

She stopped sobbing as abruptly as she had started, though the tears still ran down her face. "I'll go after him," she said. "I'll find his place in Dunham. I'll explain to him—about the lies. He'll believe me. I'll make him believe me. I've always been too proud to explain—and this is what it's brought me! I won't be too proud now." She groped distractedly about her, seeking something. "My bonnet," she said.

"Oh, Mistress," groaned Kristin; for the bonnet was still tied around Lysbet's neck.

She would not have reached Dunham before nightfall if Farmer Cottard had not stopped to give her a ride in his wagon. She had saved his wife from birthing fever last year; he was mutely and stubbornly decent to her whenever he had the opportunity.

It was a relief that he was not a talker. She could cling to the jolting seat and close her eyes, running through what she would say again and again. The litany made her almost sick. She was terrified that Thursis would not listen. Her brains seemed to be shaking with the wagon, swimming with the dust and heat that rose from the yellow road.

Cottard set her down in the village of Dunham and she asked her way. Thursis's house was another mile, not on the high road, but on the crossroad to Stetton. She tried to count her steps to ease the pain of the anticipation, to drown out the pleas that rang in her head; but she could not concentrate for more than twenty or thirty paces. She tried to look about her, and she noticed a high growth of wild hops hanging over a ditch; but then the rest was a blur.

After a time she came along some fine hayfields. She remembered what Betty Moschus had said, and knew this was the place. There was the stone barn. Once she was sure, she saw little else. She went through the gate and up the lane to the yard.

He was just coming out of the barn with a bucket in each hand. He went to the well and drew water, not seeing her as she came up; then he turned about and started. He scowled bitterly.

"What have you come for?" he said.

"To explain," she answered. Her voice was cracked with fear, with the dust of the road, and with hard thirst. But he did not offer her so much as a handful of water.

"I've had all the explaining about you I need," he said. "Get out."

"You heard lies—all lies. Let me explain!"

"Are you calling your neighbors liars? Are they all liars? Is every man jack and woman up your way a boldfaced liar? I don't think so."

She made a hoarse, almost inaudible noise of anguish, deep in her throat. It was so pathetic that he paused, if only to glare at her again. "So who is this chit you live with?" he said. "This—this Kristin girl?"

"She's my oldest and dearest friend," said Lysbet.

"Dearest, I'll bet!" he sneered.

"My *friend!* My *friend!*" she cried. "She's only my friend! When she was four years old I saved her from drowning. She had fallen into a well—we were playing, about a dozen of us children—she was a neighbor boy's little sister and she tagged along. She was such a sorry little thing—she had never spoken up to that time and she never bothered us; she just wanted to be there. We were playing by the edge of the well, and one of the boys bumped her in by accident. It was horrible—seeing her fall, the look on her face, hearing the splash—and then nothing, just silence from the well, no splashing, no crying. I couldn't bear it. I took the rope and threw it in; then I slid down—my hands were burned, I remember—"

She looked at them now, holding them out before her, palms up, as if the stripes of blood lay still fresh upon them.

"It was horrible," she said again. "Imagine, for a child—going down in a dark well, never knowing if you would be saved. It was not a deep one, but it seemed deep to me; and there was a drought, so when I reached the bottom I found I could just keep my chin above water if I stood on tiptoe. And she had given up, given up already, until she saw me and felt me. Then she cried out. It was the first time anyone had ever heard her speak. She tried to climb up on my head, and somehow I held her up until my father came. I hardly remember how we got out after that."

She was holding her throat as if the fear of that day was in it still; as if she were still down in the dark well with Kristin, waiting for a man to come and pull her up. But still the story she had rehearsed in her mind came pouring out.

"After that she never wanted to leave me. She would come over after breakfast and follow me wherever I went. She waited outside the schoolhouse. She wanted to carry my books; she wanted to do my chores; she wanted to brush my hair. She was like a dog, faithful every minute, faithful to the death. For a long while I was the only person she would talk to. Once, I remember, someone came into her house and stole something when her parents were way; they had to call me over to get her to tell who it was.

"And later, when I was about twelve, her house burned down. Everyone was killed—father, mother, sisters, brothers—and she would have been killed too, but I woke up in the middle of the night and saw the glow of the flames on the ceiling of my room, coming from across the way, and I shook my father awake, and he ran over, barefoot through the snow. The whole house was in flames, but the little lean-to part in back where she slept was only beginning to catch, and he broke through the window and pulled her out, all bloody with cuts from the glass and half-dead from the smoke.

"After that her kin tried to take her, but she kept running away and coming back to be with me. Finally my parents took her in.

"She worshipped me. When I was only fifteen she heard someone call me 'the little mistress' jokingly, and after that she called me 'Mistress.' That's what I was to her. I was everything. She thought only about what I needed, what I wanted, what she could do to help me. Many a time I've scolded her for suffering cold or hunger when she thought it would help me. And she's still like that now. She'd die for me if I snapped my fingers."

He was standing still by the well, transfixed by her story and by her urgency, but the hard, angry, cheated look had not left his face. She hurried on with what she was saying, wondering how she could make it all clear.

"My parents died when I was twenty. My oldest brother came into the place. He brought a wife in, and started looking for a husband for me. His wife—she didn't like me. She was the one who started saying ugly things. That frightened all the men away. So there I was—I had nowhere to go, and no one to marry. Finally my grandfather died, my mother's father. He and I had always been close, and he left his place to me. My brothers were angry—they thought they should have had the place; my sisters were jealous, because their husbands wanted it. So they told the lies too.

"It's been seven years I've been on the place now, just me and Kristin. It's been hard—bitter hard, and lonely, seeing your youth go by, knowing all your neighbors hate you, even when you give them the poultices that ease their aches and the brews that draw off the pain inside them. And all because of a lie!"

She paused for breath, and he spoke out at once.

"Is it a lie, then, that you and that woman are—" He groped for a word, and then spat it out with a kind of horror—"lovers?"

"It's a lie," she said flatly.

"I don't believe you," he said, just as flatly.

"Why not?" she said, beginning to weep. "I swear to you by God, by all that I love, all that I know, I have never lain with that woman. Never."

She did not know what else to say. She waited, wringing her hands, watching the scowl on his face.

"They tell me she looks at you with lust—that she can't hide it. What about that? Is that true?"

"I wouldn't call it that. I wouldn't call it lust."

"Oh? What would you call it, then?"

"Longing for acceptance. I'd call it that." She drew herself up, almost shook herself. "I won't lie to you," she said. "Kristin loves me. But it isn't like that. She would love me forever if she could. If you'd let her."

He uttered a cry of revulsion. "Be gone!" he said. "Don't bring your filthy tales around here!"

"For the love of God," she begged him, "Will you listen to me? Will you listen to what I'm saying? I've never done that with her. I've never lain with anyone, man or woman. Why won't you listen to me?"

"Why *should* I listen to you!" he shouted, now incensed. He threw down the buckets and strode forward a step, almost menacingly. "You made a fool of me! You made a fool of *me!* Every man at that raising was snickering in his sleeve when he found out I'd set my eyes on an unnatural woman—when he found out I'd kissed one!" He rubbed the back of his hand violently over his lips, as if in an attempt to wipe away an indelible stain. "I kissed one!" he said again. "And where else have your lips been, Miss Pure and Holy?"

"Listen to me!" she shouted.

"No! No! Why should *I* listen to *you?* Every farmer's daughter in this county is willing to listen to *me*. And by God, they're all younger than you, too! I've got the finest barn in six towns, and good land, a good home. Why should I talk to a woman with an evil name?"

Her cheeks burned, paled and burned. She was standing very tall, and had Kristin been there, she would have been frightened by the look in Lysbet's eyes.

"Yes," said Lysbet suddenly. "Why should you listen to me? You're just another one of the great, stupid boys who bump little girls down the well and then stand around looking foolish and doing nothing. When have you ever reached out to help someone? When have you ever risked more than a day's worth of sweat for your neighbors?—And even then you only do it because you know they'll be obligated to repay it. You have your chance to have a woman who will work like a horse for you—a woman with a back like a wagon spring, a hand that can heal, and a head for figures—and wide hips, by God, to bring you forth children. What's more, she brings with her another just like her, willing to work the flesh off her hands at your bidding just to be with me.—What am I talking about? You're throwing away *love*. Did you ever consider it? Did you ever consider the difference between a wife who loves you and some wench who wants your well? Why should such a man as you listen to me? And why should such a woman as I bother to talk to a man like you? Be damned to you, you and your farm! Be damned to you, you and your young wife! I'm better off to have escaped you, you and all your kind!"

He was so furious now that it was all he could do to contain himself. She turned on her heel and left him seething with rage.

The lane, the gate, the miles faded away without her noticing. She held her hands clenched before her as she walked; it seemed that in one she held her fiery pride, and in the other her chilly sorrow.

She did not reach home that night, although she trudged on by moonlight. She would have been very hungry, except that she knew where to look for wild food, which she snatched out of the earth in a blind stupor; she drank from springs she knew, and went around long ways to avoid certain farms where savage dogs were loosed by night. Before dawn she sagged to the ground at the side of the road, crawled into a thicket, and slept for a few hours, exhausted more by emotion than effort.

She came through the gate at about the same hour she had seen Thursis go by yesterday. She felt like a different woman. She knew she had been chasing her dreams, that she had known nothing about him; that he was not a man whom she could respect, not over the years, though she might have fooled herself for a good while. Better to see it all at once, completely and clearly, no matter how much it hurt.

She called to Kristin but heard no answer. She looked about. On the table was a note, folded over, with her name on the outer leaf. A pang went through her, and she sat down abruptly and reached out to pick the letter up.

Mistres—I see now that its all my falt. Ive always loved you but my love has brot you nothing but pane. Im going away. Now youll be able to find what you need. I'll serve you best this way. I beg you not to trie to find me. I'll be very carefull that as long as you live youll never see or hear from me agen.

A minute later Lysbet was running down the road toward the village, but she had to stop. Her breath was short, and her heart was beating so wildly it hurt; she was hungry, exhausted, and confused. "Kristin!" she called, as she halted, one shaking hand on her breastbone. But of course there was no answer, except for the droning of insects and the faint whisper of a breeze stirring among the rows of corn in the fields.

4

She hunted for Kristin for three weeks. Nowhere did she find a trace of her. No one had seen her; she must have traveled by night and hidden by day. No one could provide a clue even as to which direction she had gone.

Finally Lysbet came back to the farm, hoping to find her there. But the place was just as she had left it. The door was on the latch, the butter had spoiled in the churn, the house was resoundingly empty.

*Maybe she'll come back,* thought Lysbet.

But she did not. Not through that summer, nor the fall, nor the winter. Spring, too, came, summer again.

Lysbet lived as before, only now the work was harder, the days and evenings lonelier. She saw Thursis passing through the village once; they both grew hot with anger and looked away. She heard that he married a girl from up his way, sometime in the spring. She did not care, not even enough to curse him anymore. *So be it,* she said. *Let him make someone else happy, as happy as she's likely to be.*

One day she was down in the thyme again. She was out of sorts, but then again, she was always out of sorts since Kristin had gone. A bee stung her, that was how out of sorts she was; she had not been stung for years, and she knew it was only because she was preoccupied and clumsy, and had seized a stalk in which a bee had just landed. She pulled the stinger out by scraping it with the edge of her nail, and decided to finish her culling before she went back to put a poultice on the hurt.

She heard a wagon on the road and flushed, remembering last year. But it was Cottard. His wife sat beside him, and his many children were swaying in the box, staring at her pop-eyed. She thought she heard one of them murmur something about a witch as they passed. Cottard's wife kept her gaze averted—this woman Lysbet had saved from death; but Cottard nodded to her and touched his hat.

As they went beyond her the wagon slowed and a short distance down the road came to a complete stop. She could hear the woman protesting in urgent undertones; she caught the words "the children." But Cottard shook off her disagreement finally, handed her the reins, and climbed down out of the seat.

She stood in the middle of the thyme, waiting for him to come to her. He took his own time, not hurried by the thought that his wife would reproach him and sulk against him for a day or two for his willfulness in this. He was doing what was right.

Lysbet was curious. She had never heard him say more than four or five words together. He leaned on the fence and looked at her evenly, gently.

"Heard tell some'at about that girl you used to live with," he said. He stopped and waited for a response, but she could not speak. Perhaps that was all the response he needed.

"Was up Stetton way. Man up there has a big dairy. Has a new milkmaid; been there about a year. Hair the color of corn silk. Always moonin' about, never talks to nobody. Call her Christine. The man and his wife, they work her pretty hard."

"What's the man's name?"

"Dunno. Service, somethin' like that. Ask for the big dairy. Stetton folk'll know."

She came close to the fence. He did not shy away, but stood staunchly, not judging her.

"Cottard, you're a good man. There aren't too many of your kind hereabout."

"Folks jist talk, Miss Lysbet. Every idle word breaks a man's back and a woman's heart. That's what I say."

"Thank you, Cottard."

He touched his hat again and went back to his fidgeting family.

This time she planned her journey better. She took food and a bottle filled with water. Into the basket she threw some bundles of the fresh thyme she had been cutting; if anyone saw her, they would think she was going about her business. She closed up the house and told her neighbor she would not be coming by for milk. Then, before dawn the next morning, she began the walk to Stetton.

She had to go through Dunham. Not only that, she had to take the crossroad past Thursis's place. As she passed the long frontage of his land she had cause to think over the entire misadventure again. Now it seemed incredible that she could have been so desperate to entrust her happiness to someone else, or that she could have gone to beg and plead with him to give up his prejudice against her, and against Kristin.

She discovered that Stetton was dairy country. She had never known that before. When she asked in the village, she found that there were no fewer than three Christines who were milkmaids on the outlying farms. Eventually someone was able to identify two of them by family; the third one, who worked for a man named Case, he did not know; he thought she was from away.

But this Christine was not the right one. Lysbet actually found the farm and talked to the girl. Farmer Case happened along, and he thought maybe there was a girl by that name on the other side of Stetton, working for a man named Seris.

It was evening of the second day before Lysbet found the place. She was walking, footsore and anxious, along a high road among hills, and came around a bend to find a vast farm spread out below her, with pasture and woodlot, a great farmhouse, and a series of barns, dairies, springhouses, chicken coops, and miscellaneous outbuildings. As she stood amazed at the size of the place, she saw a throng of milkmaids come out of the distant barn and scatter among the various houses.

She went a little farther down the road. A small wood had been allowed to grow up here, and she turned off the track into its shadow. Sinking to the ground, she rested for a few minutes, ate and drank, and splashed water on her face.

The sun began to set. The farm below the hill was painted gold, as if in allegory of its busy prosperity. Activity gradually ceased. Lysbet sat, watching the place. She puzzled over why she waited, she invented a dozen reasons; but she realized that there was a new knowledge, a new feeling tugging at her that she was still trying to brush away. She sat and tried to let the feeling come, whatever it was.

A door slammed at the side of the farmhouse below. A figure came away from the house; Lysbet knew at once that it was Kristin. She walked directly out of the yard, heading straight for the hilltop where Lysbet sat. A woman opened the door behind her and bawled the name "Christine," but Kristin pretended not to hear and kept walking.

Lysbet moved sideways into the shelter of a viburnum. No one could see her here, but she could watch Kristin come closer.

She knew all of a sudden that this was a nightly ritual with Kristin. This hilltop lay in the long line between the Seris farm and Lysbet's; from this height Kristin could look out over several of the many hills that intervened between her and her mistress.

Seris and his wife may have been working her hard, but she did not look broken by the labor. She looked healthy and strong. All the same, there was a listlessness in her step; she wandered up the slope, planting one foot and pulling the other up behind her, one after another. She did not seem to see where she was going, or how the sun lit the grass with gold just as it lit her golden head.

*Dear God,* thought Lysbet suddenly, *what have I done with this great gift you gave me? You gave a life into my care; she was child, sister, friend, servant, consoler, nurse to me. She loved me when my brothers and sisters cast me out, when the world whispered against me, when I broke her heart chasing a fool of a man with the mind of a boy. Have I ever really been happy but with her? If I hadn't had my heart set on a love I could not have, I would have been perfectly happy years ago. I might have given my love to her and been satisfied and complete.*

She felt this truth come into her fully; and for the first time in her life she lived fully in the present, with her present love, needing no promises for the future. Her long seeking after immediacy came to fruition.

She trembled. She seized the thyme in the basket and crushed it in her hands, pressed the wilted leaves to her throat and her cheeks as a kind of anointing at the beginning of a new life, a real and true life.

Kristin's path led her near the thicket. When she was close, Lysbet rose to her feet so that Kristin could see her.

At first Kristin seemed not to believe her eyes. Stumbling forward, she put out a hand, as if Lysbet would blow away, as if she might catch only a wisp of mist, a seeming.

They met and embraced.

Lysbet kissed Kristin's face again and again, while Kristin wept and murmured "Mistress! Mistress!" over and over.

Suddenly Kristin held herself away. "What about Thursis?" she asked.

Lysbet smiled.

"He married someone else."

"Oh—"

"Don't be sorry. I'm not."

Kristin looked at her, marveling. "You're not?"

"No."

"Why not?" asked Kristin.

"Because I have to love the one God gave me to love."

"What do you mean?"

"You should say, 'Whom do you mean?' Because I mean you."

"Me? But what about . . . marriage?"

"If that comes to me, ever, it will come to me. But you I will always love. I will not abandon you, no matter what. And you must never run away from me again. You must promise me that."

"But I mustn't take your dream away from you," said Kristin. "And by staying with you, I do that."

"No," said Lysbet. "Let us hold to this first. We are friends until death, and we shall be together despite all."

And she embraced Kristin again and held her.

After a minute, a minute of silence and wonderment, Kristin said, "Dear God, is this true?"

She pressed her face against the side of Lysbet's neck, drawing in a deep breath and laughing softly. "Thyme!" she exclaimed.

# Jack

The one best place to bury a good dog is in the heart of its master.

—Anonymous

The heat moved over the land in swells; occasionally it was modulated by a breeze that seemed to have found its way over the hills from the sea.

Dale was sitting in the shade of the old fir tree by the house, waiting for his wife and daughter and the dog to come.

He put his head back against the crusty bark of the fir. His brain seemed both light and heavy—so light that he wished to prop his head to hold it from wobbling, so heavy that he had to concentrate to keep it from drooping.

He saw his wife first, her head above the gaps in the hedgerow. Her hair was golden—that was the color that caught the light at this distance, though he knew there was gray among that gold. As she came around the last of the hedge he saw Cootha beside her, pacing along with that childish step that was like a heartbeat that skips for joy. Cootha's head, too, was golden, all light curls piled one over the other. She sometimes pushed and prodded at the basket his wife carried; she knew what was in it; she was only six, and her thoughts were on that. *A good place for them to be,* he thought.

And then last of all came Jack, the dog. He, too, was golden, of a pale gold, as if each individual thread of his coat had been spun of gleaming metal, and yet spun also of air, infinitely soft. He was gold from head to tail, except for his face, which was a white mask showing his age. He disliked the heat, under that heavy coat; he followed his people with a dragging step, his body reluctant, but his will insisting.

It struck Dale then how they, all three of them, were golden; and he, up here on the hill waiting, was dark. As if that somehow explained why they had gone apart from him; because they were alike and he different. But it was a foolish thought, a weak thought, and he forgot it. He would never raise any such fancied barrier between Cootha and himself; she would be his child, always, and his home would be hers, always, no matter that she did not live in it.

He watched the dog laboring up the hill. He knew Jack would be thinking about water, about the bowl of water in the corner of the kitchen where it had always been. You could not always tell what a dog was thinking—usually they were not thinking about anything—but you could always tell when they were thinking about water, just the way they moved. It was not just the lolling tongue, because the tongue would still hang like that when they had filled their bellies with water and lay panting, waiting for their agony to pass. A thirsty dog had its own peculiar look.

He knew Jack's looks. He had known him from a puppy; Arielle's parents had bought the dog a few days after the wedding; and Jack had so taken to his wife that they had given up their claim to him.

She had loved the dog more than she had loved Dale. That was the long and short of it. Dale knew that; had always known it; but had not always been as free of bitterness about it as he was now.

Arielle was afraid of everyone. Afraid people were judging her; afraid that she could never measure up to some secret standard they would not let her know or see, except as it was reflected in their contempt.

He had spent thirteen years trying to persuade her that he loved her as she was. He had failed, because, not loving herself, she could not understand how anyone else could love her. In her own wounded judgment she was condemned; she would not believe his affection.

But Jack did not judge. She knew that. He would sit beside her and rest his head on her lap, staring vaguely into the middle distance with his liquid, brown eyes, while she stroked his fur. He would need nothing more, and she nothing more from him. It was love without demand or complication. It was the only love she was capable of receiving, and as the years had told, the only love she was capable of giving.

Dale had refused to be jealous of the dog. He valued his love too highly to weigh it in the same scale as that of an animal. Even now he clung to this belief in the superiority of his affection, even though it had been so thoroughly and conclusively rejected.

It was Dale who had taken care of Jack, strangely enough. Who had fed him, walked with him in all weathers, carried him in and out and up and down in his sicknesses (of which the dog had had many). Perhaps he did it to prove that he was not jealous. Perhaps he did it because he knew that his wife did not know how to care for anyone, not even herself.

Perhaps he did it because, even in the beginning, he had pitied them all.

It was in his nature to love whom he served; and he had come to love Jack, even though he received little attention from the beast beyond a faint wag of recognition now or then, or a peremptory bark when some canine schedule had been overlooked. And now, as he watched the dog struggling up the hill, his affection brought ready tears to his eyes.

*This is the last time, old boy,* he thought. *You'll never have to climb that hill again.*

He could not bear to watch them now. He set his head back tightly against the bark and looked at the fair-weather clouds moving slowly in the summer sky. He felt broken; as if some loving mechanism in his soul had been overwound and now was compressed under great tension; as if it would never come unstuck; as if he would never take a wife again, or love another dog. He felt that his remembrance of the years and years of profitless servitude to these two beings he had loved would always recur and prevent him from commitment. He would remember how there had been no reward, no answering affection, in spite of all his care.

When Arielle and Cootha had come into the dooryard, and Jack was still catching up, Dale rose and greeted them. Arielle smiled wanly, her grief evident in the dark hollows beneath her blue eyes. He pursued Cootha where she darted about and hugged and kissed her.

"We brought cake," she said.

"Sharing food together is a part of mourning," said Arielle, as if repeating something someone had told her. Then she was struck with doubt. "Is it all right?"

"Of course," said Dale. "I made a little something myself."

"Did you finish digging the grave?"

"It's all ready. I took the stone over there, too."

"What stone, Dad?" Cootha wanted to know.

"The big one we picked out. Remember?"

"Oh, the gravestone."

A few days ago they had chosen a large flat stone from one of the walls that crossed the fields. They had found a place for the grave, too, under a huge, dense stand of lilacs by the edge of the road. Jack had been with them then; he had sat down abruptly on the spot they had picked, staring into the shadows of the lilacs, as if testing the place.

Now Arielle came close to Dale impulsively. "Thank you for doing everything," she said. "I couldn't have done it by myself. I just couldn't have."

"It was only right," he said, demurring. But he was moved by her words. It was seldom that she had thanked him for anything.

By now Jack had entered the yard and stood panting and weary in the sun. Dale went to him and patted him, sinking his fingers into his thick fur. The animal looked up at him briefly; one eye was still clear and wide, but the other was swollen shut by the great bony tumor that had taken over the left side of his face under the skin. The growth had been increasing daily; now it seemed it must be pressing tightly on the eyeball under the puffed lid; in the way of dogs, however, Jack showed no pain.

"You're thirsty, boy," he said. Then: "Come inside, everyone."

He led them into the dark house. The air was only slightly cooler here. Jack went straight to his accustomed corner and drank the water from the bowl there as if he meant to bloat himself. When he was finished, Dale refilled it. The scent of the cold, fresh water was too tempting, and Jack went back to the bowl and drank again.

"That's right, boy," said Dale. "Enjoy it."

"He dug a hole under the bushes out in front of the house this morning," said Arielle. "I let him out and then I looked for him. I finally found him lying in there, all dirty and hot." She wrung her hands nervously, looking at Jack as he finally moved away from the bowl and stood waiting to see what his people would do. Cootha seemed to be moving in orbit around their grief, unable to feel with them, but curious about the novelty of death; she went here and there around the kitchen, even into the other rooms, always returning.

"I think we're doing the right thing, don't you?" asked Arielle, without pausing for an answer. "That thing has gotten so big . . . it must be hurting him. It's so close to his eye now. You can feel it under the skin. It's all hard and bony. We could wait, but he'd be miserable where we're going. And what would I do in the city when he died? And he might suffer so much—"

They had had this conversation many times before. "It's the right thing," said Dale with gentle finality. "Don't think about that anymore, don't worry about that. It's not just the right thing, it's the only thing we can do."

"But it seems so hard, when he's so healthy in every other way. He's old, but he still enjoys life. Last night

I let him out and he sat in the yard for an hour, just sniffing all the smells the night air was bringing to him."

It was her way to knot herself into a tangle of guilt and self-blame. He knew from his marriage with her that there was no way he could cut her out of that, no way to reassure her absolutely, even in a case like this, when the choice was clear, even though it was grim.

"Everyone has to die of something. Maybe it's a blessing that for him it's something like this that doesn't cripple him. Something that lets him enjoy himself to the last minute. It would be awful if he couldn't walk or if he was sick and wretched."

"Yes," she said. She seemed a little comforted by this way of looking at things.

"Here, Jacko," he said. "I've got some cheese saved for you." He took some morsels from a plate on the table and fed them to the dog one by one. Jack took each piece in his gentle mouth, then bolted it down with greedy zest.

"Someone's here," said Cootha, running suddenly into the room.

Dale and Arielle looked at each other.

"I'll tell her we'll be right out," said Arielle.

"All right," he said.

"Where shall we do it? It's so hot out there."

"But he'd rather be outside. He loves the outdoors so much. What about in the shade, under the big fir tree?"

She nodded her agreement and went away to talk to the vet. In a minute she was back. "She said not to hurry. Whenever we're ready."

Without a word Dale and Arielle knelt by Jack and patted him. Cootha flitted out of the room.

The dog stood passively beneath their attention. He was so real, his body so warm and solid; he was panting lightly, and he shifted a little.

*In a few minutes,* thought Dale as he tried to grasp what was happening, tried to arrest and retain this moment in his memory, *he won't be moving, he won't be breathing. The life, whatever that is, will be gone from him, and nothing will be able to bring it back. This creature I love will never walk with me again.*

He was weeping silently. He saw that Arielle was weeping too. Suddenly she caught at his hand where it lay over the back of the dog's neck. She clung to it.

"Don't worry," he said. "It'll be all right."

It would not be all right; what he meant was that it would be right. That was the only consolation. Nothing was all right, nothing would ever be all right anymore.

"I just don't want to lose everything," she wept. "Everything all at once."

*Everything?* he reflected bitterly. *You're taking Cootha away. Is that losing everything? If you're so sorry to be losing me, why don't you stay? Why don't you come back? Why are you still going away?*

But aloud he answered, "It would be worse to watch him suffer."

"I know," she said. She let go of his hand.

Cootha reappeared. "Come say goodbye," Arielle told her.

She, too, came and patted the big dog. "Goodbye, Jack," she said.

Her first word, spoken when she was eight or nine months old, had been "Dak." She used to shriek with laughter when confronted by his furry face as she toddled around the house. As she had grown up the pictures she drew had always been of the house, her father and mother, herself, and Jack beside them, with a brilliant rainbow of peace and love overhead. She was a precocious writer; the dog's name had been one of the first she could spell.

Now there was a long silence as they all patted him together. Dale felt the futility of their affection suddenly, but he ignored that new and troubling thought.

"Well," he said, in a hoarse voice.

They rose to their feet.

"You remember what we talked about?" asked Arielle anxiously.

"Yes," he said. They had agreed that Cootha should not actually see the vet give the dog the poison. Dale would bring her inside when that was happening. "Did you tell the vet?"

"Yes. She knows all about it."

"Let's go, then," said Dale.

"Come on, Jack," said Arielle faintly. He stepped after her. Dale knew that the dog would never suspect, not even in the last moment before the poison took hold. He trusted them absolutely; fear of death was not in his thoughts.

They went out of the house. The vet was waiting. She seemed outside the circle drawn by their grief, despite the kindliness and compassion that was written in her features. Dale greeted her.

"Does the little one know what's going on?" she asked.

"Yes," said Arielle. "We've explained everything."

"You understand that this will be better for him?" the vet asked Cootha.

Cootha hung back shyly, not knowing how to answer.

"It won't hurt him," added the vet. "It won't hurt him at all. It will be just like falling asleep."

Cootha nodded a little.

Arielle had brought an old blanket with her. This she took to the shade of the big fir tree. They spread it out; when she knelt on it, Jack immediately followed her and lay down beside her, setting his golden head in her lap. The vet made a few preparations.

"Are you ready?" asked Dale.

"Yes," said the vet.

"Come on, Cootha," said Dale. "Pat him one more time."

They both stroked his fur. It was impossible to conceive that in a minute or two this animal they loved would be dead.

"Come back inside," he told Cootha.

He took her by the hand and they went back across the dooryard and into the house.

"It will just be a minute," he told her, as they paused inside the door. He looked toward the fir tree at intervals.

He saw the vet stand; heard the words "That's it."

"All right," he told Cootha. "We can go out again."

As he crossed the dooryard again and saw Jack stretched out motionless across Arielle's lap, he felt his life had slammed headlong into some immovable barrier. Until now everything that had gone wrong could still have been undone; or at least he could in some part of his thought still pretend that what was good in the old life they had had could be recalled. This was the first of the unalterable choices that were to now to be made.

He knelt by Jack again and set his fingers deep into the golden fur. *It's still soft,* he thought in bitter amazement, as though death should have instantly coarsened it, as though the fur were in itself living. He was weeping and all he could see was a golden blur.

Cootha knelt beside him. As she looked on Jack's body, the finality of the event was borne in upon her; and for a moment she was not a child, but simply a mortal confronting loss and death. She sobbed, instantly and grievously; and Dale held her instead of Jack.

"He didn't feel anything," said the vet again. "It's better for him now. He won't hurt anymore."

In a few minutes the intensity of Cootha's grief ebbed. Life stretched out too far before her; she could not hold the immediacy of death in her mind for long.

The vet was going. Dale rose and thanked her, but he could not put into words his thanks for her kindness and discretion.

Then they were alone, the three of them; one less than they had been.

They patted him still, for quite some time, in silence. Finally Dale spoke.

"He knew we loved him. That's the important thing."

"Yes," said Arielle.

"Every minute is a chance," said Dale. "To show your love, or to feel it. You have to take those chances; otherwise you look back and you're sorry."

"Yes," said Arielle; but he did not know if she appreciated the larger meaning of his words.

"Well," he said, after an interval.

"Shall we bury him now?" asked Arielle. She wiped the tears away from her cheeks with her fingertips and then covered her eyes again.

"Yes," he said.

She held up Jack's head so that she could stand. Dale brought a cart, two shovels, and an iron rake. And water, spring water; he knew they would all need it.

They wrapped the body in the blanket. Dale lifted it into the cart. "He's so heavy," he said in surprise; for a limp body feels heavier than a quick one.

They went out into the field. At the lilacs Dale stopped the cart.

Arielle looked into the grave. "What a lot of work!" she exclaimed. She looked gratefully at Dale; he felt the sweetness of the glance.

"Well, I wanted everything to be the best for the old man," he said. "All we have to do is get him down into it."

Now the body seemed lighter, as if already its corporeal grossness were dissolving, leaving only a golden husk. He put the form in the blanket at the edge of the grave, descended into the earth, and then lowered the burden down onto the cool clay.

Arielle and Cootha hung over the grave, watching. He pulled back the corner of the blanket to see the golden head one last time. "Goodnight, old dog," he said. "Sleep well. Sweet dreams."

"Goodbye, Jack," said Cootha.

"Goodbye," said Arielle.

He ran his fingers through Jack's fur, feeling keenly that he would never be able to do so again. Then he closed the flap of the blanket.

"Wait," said Arielle. "Let's put flowers in with him."

He waited while they plucked wildflowers and brought them in bunches; then he tucked them in around the blanketed form.

He climbed out. "What do we do now?" asked Arielle. She had always had a pathetic way of appealing for guidance even when there were no options.

"We fill it in," he said, as gently as he could.

He fetched a shovel and began putting soil back in the grave.

"You don't have to do all that yourself," said Arielle. She took another shovel and began helping him. They filled in the corners of the grave first, as if that would ease the burden on Jack; or perhaps because they could not endure to cast dirt on him.

Dale's head ached from the weeping and the sun and the heat. He had to stop frequently to drink water; and still he felt that his insides were drying up and shrinking tight. Gradually the flowers disappeared, then the blanket.

Dale felt that he and the woman who worked beside him were burying their marriage—the living, golden spirit of it. The thirteen years they had lived together; plans; memories; the sacrifices they had cheerfully made to begin a life together and to continue it; all the things that Arielle's decision had put to sleep forever.

The one thing they were not burying was their love for Cootha. That was one thing they would never forget or regret.

Cootha insisted on helping with the shoveling. He was proud of her: she seemed so strong, spiritually and physically, as she carried her mite of stone and earth to the grave, balancing a shovel longer than she was.

When they almost had the grave filled he called a halt and set back in place the great squares of sod he had cut from the spot before he began digging. They fit perfectly. The grave almost disappeared; in a month or two the seams where the turf had been cut would heal, and only the stone would mark the place where the golden body lay.

It seemed horrible, wrong, that the creature that had once frisked in the clear air under the open sky should be pinned forever under the enormous weight of the damp earth; that those ribs that only a few minutes ago had been heaving with breath should now be crushed. He could not bear to think of it.

He brought the stone over. It was roughly oval, about a yard across, and about two inches thick: an odd stone to find among these hills, which were littered with boulders anciently rounded and broken by water and ice. He had already explained to Cootha that it would not be upright like the graves in the cemetery, but flat on the grave; and thus he set it down. They consulted about how it should lie; then he cut out the sod slightly to fit it, so that it snugged into the earth. He took some painful pleasure in the neatness of the work.

"It's supposed to say his name," said Cootha.

Here was a detail they had not discussed; Dale could not think of any way to explain this away.

"I'll write it on there," she suggested.

Dale could see Arielle was torn—she thought the stone should not be defaced; and yet she saw how Cootha needed this to complete the fitness of the rite.

"All right," said Arielle.

Cootha took a stone and scratched in large letters across the gravestone: *JACK.*

He saw that the letters would soon fade, worn away by the weather; perhaps this knowledge soothed Arielle, or perhaps she accepted Cootha's offering.

He was exhausted. The manual labor was nothing, but the emotional work was wearing heavily upon him. Arielle, too, seemed almost stupified by grief. He put the shovels in the cart.

But Cootha was not finished. "We have to pray," she said.

"All right," said Arielle.

"How should we do it?" asked Dale.

"Everybody kneel by the grave."

Obediently they joined her. Dale felt that this, too, was a last time; that never would they pray together again.

"Do we pray out loud, or do we pray by ourselves?"

"By ourselves."

They folded their hands and bowed their heads.

As he thought of Jack, kneeling there in the grass, in the thick silence of the summer heat, he felt that in the death of the dog there was some answer for him, some lesson for him, if he could only see it and learn from it.

*God,* he prayed, *help me to understand how this is a blessing.*

Cootha looked up with a radiant smile. The rite had been satisfied.

Arielle spoke, borne up by Cootha's happiness. "He's just running up to the gates of heaven now," she said.

They all smiled at the fiction. It was a soothing one.

For several hours they sat in the kitchen. They had coffee and tea and pieces of Arielle's cake, as well as some bread Dale had made. For Cootha there was also lemonade, as much as she wanted to drink.

Even in their grief there was gladness that the painful acts had been accomplished; they relaxed in this false relief as though in the lull of a great hurricane. For a little time they were a family again.

They talked of Jack. The things he had done, both gentle and naughty, both doglike and human. They talked of where Arielle and Cootha would be living; how they would be moving in the next few days. They talked of things they had done together, man, woman, and child.

As Dale ate the cake Arielle had made he looked at her and listened to her. She was beautiful, as beautiful as she had ever been. He doubted she would ever find someone who could think her as beautiful as he did; for no one would ever look at her with the eyes of thirteen years of their love. To him, he knew, she would always have been beautiful, however age changed her; but now her beauty had become but a sweetness that must fade in the senses. The tea, as he drank it after the sweetness of the cake, tasted bitter by comparison.

Then it was five o'clock. The day and its events had rushed upon them too quickly, before they could be ready; now it was rushing away; now Arielle and Cootha would be leaving.

As Arielle rose to go, Dale felt suddenly how none of the choices were his. Arielle had all the choices—to stay, to go, to love or not. He had no power over her, if his affection for her meant nothing to her. And she was proving that it was not enough.

"Well," she said.

"Getting late," he said, forcing his voice to sound cheerful. *I'm forty*, he thought. *From now on it will always be getting late.*

"Keep some of the cake," she said.

"No—"

"We can never eat that much," she said; and as he looked at how much was left, he realized the absurdity of protesting. She cut a large portion of it and transferred it to one of his plates.

He followed them out into the sunlight. The heat was still intense. The sun still had hours to tend until setting.

Cootha began to run about as she had earlier, distracted by her favorite things—the swing under the firs, her collection of stones in the hollow of a tree. For a minute more Dale stood with Arielle on the crest of the hill.

"Thank you again for everything," she said.

"Don't thank me," he said. "You don't have to thank me."

He felt hurt now by her insistence.

"Take care of his grave for me," she said.

*For you? For you?* he thought. *Why just for you? Why not for my sake too? Did I love him, did I take care of him all those years, just for you? Is everything just for you? Are you the only one who loves, who mourns, who feels?*

"It's so hard—going home," she said, "when I know he won't be there to greet me."

*And when you're gone,* thought Dale, *I'll go back into my empty house alone.*

"But it's better this way," she said. "There's a will, there's a reason for everything."

"Yes," he said. "I think . . ." and he hesitated, reflecting on all he was losing, and how he had felt during the months of their separation that he could never take another wife, ever have another dog, again.

And now he saw the blessing in Jack's death. It put him face to face with what he had loved; and it taught him that the bitterness of love does not last, but the sweetness remains forever. He would forget, someday, that the dog had not loved him; but he would remember always how that golden fur felt in his fingers. He felt suddenly that he could have another dog again. *My dog,* he thought. *A dog that loves* me.

And the blessing in losing Arielle? That he could find his way out of the maze that their marriage had been. That he could love and be loved as he deserved. *A wife,* he thought. *A wife who loves* me.

This choice was in his power: the choice to believe in love, to love someone else, to try again. It was the only choice Arielle could not take away from him, not unless he let her. He had been like her for too long, pathetically inquiring of God what his options were, when in truth there was only one choice to make.

"What I feel, losing Jack," he said, almost incoherently, "is that it's worth it. The love is worth all the pain."

"Of course," she said. "Love is everything. Love is all there is. What else is there to live for?"

He stared at her, amazed even after all these years by this paradox of a woman. *So why are you throwing love away?* he wanted to ask.

But he knew that she would have no answer to his question; that she was still wandering, lost, in the labyrinth of old hurts, and that his question would only baffle her.

Arielle called to Cootha.

Dale hugged the girl and kissed her. "I'll come see you again before you go," he said.

"I'm excited," she said.

"About what?" he asked.

"Moving to the city."

He managed a smile. "Good. I'm sure it will be great fun for you."

They started away down the hill. Cootha waved once, but Arielle did not look back.

*And where's the blessing in losing Cootha?* he asked God.

*Maybe it's better for Cootha,* he thought. *That would be a blessing.*

He watched as the golden curls went out of sight behind the hedge at the foot of the hill. *Yes,* he thought, *maybe there is some way that it's a blessing. Maybe time will show.*

# Likenesses

Each and all things that appear to the sight in this world are correspondences and representations, which contain in themselves truths.

—Swedenborg

"It's no use," said Aurora finally.

She cast the bucket back into the well, but heard no splash; only the thump of wood hitting mud.

"No use," repeated little Vanessa.

"No oose," echoed Stella, her smaller sister.

The two children looked at their mother with round, dark eyes, as if wondering whether they should be scared.

"I'm thirsty, Mama," said Vanessa. She was just old enough to understand the consequences of a drought.

"Don't worry, honey. We still have some water in the jar at home. We'll drink a little, and then sit on the hill and wait for Papa to come home. When he does we'll go get more water at Compton's spring."

She took a hand in each of hers and led them back up to the house. The muscles of her thighs were sore from climbing up and down this slope constantly over the past three days in an effort to coax what water she could from the lees of the well. Most times she had carried Stella, sometimes Vanessa, too. She was per-spiring; since there had been no water with which to wash, she now felt dirty; she knew there was a streak of drying mud on her cheek, but she did not have a hand free to wipe it away.

The grasses through which they walked were sere and brown. The cow lowed at her as they passed, as if begging her to notice the condition of its pasture, or reminding her that it, too, would need its ration from Compton's. *What a time to take the wagon,* she thought to herself; and then was sick of the thought, which had rung in her head dozens of times since Thor had gone away.

It truly was a bad time, though; she could not excuse it. He was overwhelmed with the struggle—with the crops that were dying in the fields; with two children irritated by the heat; with his silent wife, who knew as well as he that everything was coming apart, as surely as a wagon driver knows a wheel will break when he sees the first spoke has gone.

He had set off for Hancock. He always went there. The folks were wealthy in Hancock; it was an up-and-coming town. Thor liked just to walk around the streets, to see clean, well-dressed men and women who did not have to grub in the dirt for a living; to buy a few new things in the shops. He always came home refreshed, ready to go on for a while; so she never complained; even though he spent too much money, and left her with all the work to do.

Lately, however, his trips had seemed to leave him less and less reinvigorated. They had seemed even to be sapping his enthusiasm. He had once actually talked of moving to Hancock, although they had no money to do so, and no way to earn a living in a town.

When she and the children reached the house, she gave them as much water as they wanted, and then drank sparingly herself. She had about a half-gallon left. It was a long way to Compton's, and the horse would be tired; but unless Thor were willing to go on foot and bring back enough to tide them over, the animal could not be spared the journey.

Outside the stuffy house a cicada screamed in the stifling air. "Come on," she said quietly, shepherding the children before her.

They trooped up to the hilltop. She sank abruptly in the parched grass. When the girls started playing together to one side—forgetting to need her for a few minutes—she felt such gratitude and relief she thought for a moment she might weep.

She looked upward haggardly. The sky was not cloudless by any means. In fact it was thronged with clouds, pushing rapidly eastward in serried ranks, like the little clouds that Vanessa made out of milkweed fluff, laying them out on the tabletop in strict columns and rows.

It seemed to Aurora suddenly that her life was like those clouds. They looked so even, so ordered; but they were really just pushed at random by some upper wind, scudding on the hot air beneath them. Fair weather clouds; no rain in them. Fine, if they did not go on too long; but if they did—unbearable.

She turned her eyes away from the sky and looked to the road. Along the edge was an old cellarhole— tumbling in on itself, its granite sill showing gaps where the stone had been scavenged for other uses. *That's my life,* she thought. *The old things, the old ways I love, the things I believed in, broken, abandoned, stolen, put to wrong uses.*

She looked back at the house. Everywhere were signs that the lives of those who dwelt in it were out of control. Props held up the porch roof; shingles were nailed over the leaking window that looked out over the west; the dead fir limbs still lay around the foundation, once dark green against the snow of last winter, but now brown. *That's my life, too,* she thought. *Patched, needy, forgotten, waiting.*

And inside, the littleness and fewness of the rooms—where they lived in the kitchen, slept in the unfinished attic under sloping ceilings. Taut, spaceless, narrow. *My life,* she thought.

She shuddered as she realized what she was doing. *Don't start it again,* she told herself. Thor called this "likenessing." It was a kind of mood, a trap of thought. At times everything she looked at seemed to suggest some likeness. Sometimes it was pleasant and soothing, but other times it was hurtful, a compulsion she could not fathom or resist. On those few occasions when she did reproach Thor for his thoughtlessness, the likenesses bubbled from her lips uncontrollably. He seized on them at once, mocking them, and her protests foundered on his sarcasm.

She sometimes thought she could hardly blame him. If he had started shouting at her, babbling about how his life was like the clouds—like the grass that was parched and sere as straw—like the weathered gray stones heaved off the long lines of the pasture walls—she would have been just as confused and shocked.

She lay back in the crackling grass, closing her eyes to avoid the sight of the sky, of anything outside her that might become a likeness of her life.

A longing for sleep sponged her with its damp promise of oblivion. *I mustn't,* she thought. She knew she should sit up, or she would succumb; but she could still hear the children near her, and she told herself she would just lie quietly for a moment, just a moment.

Her sleep was disordered by her anxiety. The children's voices still came to her, drifting through her mind and then fading, returning, loud and then faint. She dreamed she was a cloud, a bit of milkweed fluff blown before a wind; she called to Thor to catch her and hold her down, but he only said it was the logical end of her likenessing. There was more, but it was all so weird and shapeless it seemed like the dreamings of a fever.

Then Vanessa was calling to her, and she woke. "Papa's here!" the child was saying.

She struggled upright, confused, her head heavy. The sky had changed while she slept; the discrete clouds had closed ranks and formed a high, leaden overcast; but not the kind that forebode rain, or at least not in their part of the country. On the road below she saw Thor urging the weary horse up the last dusty yards toward home. "Papa!" cried Stella.

He looked up and saw them. He waved cheerfully. The girls crowed enthusiastically, and Aurora made herself wave with a show of happiness, dreading the meeting, but thinking of the wagon, the horse, the water at Compton's.

"Come to the barn," she said to the girls. "We'll meet him at the barn." The children ran ahead. He always gave them extravagant presents when he returned from these trips to Hancock.

When he drew near, Aurora forgot their troubles for a moment. He looked so handsome, sitting straight up on the wagon seat, his eyes bright, smiling at the girls. But when he descended and looked at her, his smile faded.

"You're a mess," he said. "What's happened to you?" Then he turned away abruptly, laughing at the importuning children. She wiped away the tears that his hurtful words had brought to her eyes, thinking bitterly, *No kiss, no embrace.*

"Aurora," he said, "get water for the horse, will you? It needs a drink badly. So do I."

"We have none," she said. "Only about half a jar. If you can make do with just a sip, we'll give the rest to the horse and go to Compton's."

"God, woman," he said, his fine mood broken, "do you have to begin your complaining at once? Can't I have a moment to rest after my trip? Can't you see I'm tired?"

"I would have waited," she said faintly. "But you asked for water."

"Vanessa," he said, "Go to the house and get the jar. Then you can have your present."

She wanted her present first; there was negotiation that ended in Thor's displeasure and a threat to give her treat to Stella. In a minute she was back, hugging the jar in her arms, stumbling so in her eagerness that Aurora was frightened she would fall and break the crockery—and be hurt, and no water to wash the cut.

But Vanessa reached Thor without incident. He took the jar and drank off half the water.

"Thor," said Aurora reproachfully. "The horse! It's all we have!"

"There's plenty for the horse," he said. Aurora took the jar when he set it in the dust, and poured out its contents into a bucket. The horse drank off the quart, licked the bucket, and snorted, its thirst only whetted.

Meanwhile Thor was digging through his pack for the presents. For Vanessa he had brought a pencil; for Stella a dried flower. In other times these might have been received with delight; but he had spoiled the children so that now they cast their gifts on the ground and pouted, demanding better.

In her current weakness, Aurora could not brace herself to deal with this understandable rudeness; she only looked on, her lip trembling, while Thor chastised them for their ingratitude. After each outburst of their disgust, he glared at his wife, as if their bad manners were her fault.

"Don't mind them," she appealed to him finally. "They're hot and tired, and we're all thirsty. Come, Thor, we've got to go to Compton's. The horse and the cow will need water. We haven't a drop in the house."

"Let me sit a moment," he said. He went into the house abruptly, leaving them outside.

"Don't carry on so," she said gently to the girls.

"But I don't want a pencil! I want a toy!" exclaimed Vanessa.

"Look at me," said Aurora, unable to keep the bitterness out of her voice. "I didn't get what I wanted either."

This silenced them. They sensed there was some larger meaning to her words, something frightening. She regretted having spoken. She tied the reins of the horse to a post and went inside after Thor.

"What was it that you wanted, Mama?" asked Vanessa worriedly as they went into the parlor.

"Never mind, child," she said. Fortunately Thor did not notice.

He had recovered his good spirits. He was determined to revel in his trip to Hancock; they would all have to hear about it, she saw. He would do nothing for them until they had paid him the tribute of attention.

"Let me tell you about my trip," he said.

The girls sat on stools near him. Aurora settled on a chair, looking around the room vaguely, as she wondered why he had chosen this place to enforce their hearing. Then she knew: it was the best room in the house, the room most like the rooms in Hancock.

As he began his story she looked at him curiously. "Is that a new shirt you have on?" she said, interrupting him.

"That's what they're wearing nowadays," he said. "I bought three of them."

"Three?"

He nodded, heedless of any wrong.

After that she listened in a marveling stupor, almost wondering who this man was whom she had married. Or wondering why this man was so unlike the man she had married. He had not been like this then; his tastes had been simpler, his principles had been better; he had been able to discern what was appropriate and what was not. Now he had become so unlike her that their differences had become a threat to their marriage.

He told of his journey in detail; where he had stayed, the people he had seen, the shops visited; what people were saying, what new buildings were going up. The children quickly lost interest and began fretting and quarreling with each other, but Thor was so absorbed in himself that he hardly perceived them. From time to time he reproved them sharply, and then resumed his story. Once he was commenting on the wife of a man he had met and stopped what he was saying to look keenly at his own wife. "She wasn't like you, Aurora," he said.

*As if I could ever be like a Hancock woman,* she thought.

Aurora bided the end of it. At length he subsided into silence, still glowing with his recollections. She made one last effort.

"I'm glad you enjoyed your journey, Thor."

He smiled, looking into an unseen distance—still, perhaps, gazing down the main street of Hancock.

She summoned her resources, hoping to modulate her tone so that she did not seem to be nagging.

"But we need water," she said, unable to help sounding plaintive. "We should go to the spring right away. We can all go—you can tell us more on the way there."

He frowned. "The horse is too tired," he said. He now remembered that the horse had not been cared for, and went outside as abruptly as he had come in.

She followed him, and the children rushed after her, sensing that a quarrel was in the offing, clinging to her skirts. Thor immediately began taking the horse out of its traces.

"Thor! Please!" she said. "We have to have water. If we wait any longer, the horse will suffer all the more." She laid her hand on his appealingly, but he shook it off and continued unfastening the harness. She tried pointing out the only alternative. "Will you go on foot and bring back enough for us to get through till tomorrow?"

"Why don't you go?" he asked curtly.

"I'm too exhausted," she confessed. "It's too far. I could never carry enough."

"Well, I'm tired too," he responded.

She began to cry.

"What are we going to do, then?" she asked, hoping to throw the decision on his shoulders, to force him to take responsibility.

"We'll wait till tomorrow."

"We *can't* wait. What are you talking about, wait till tomorrow?"

He looked up at the overcast sky. "Looks like it might rain," he said.

"It won't rain! You know it won't. The sky has looked like that for weeks at a time this summer."

"If you want water, why don't you go down to the stream and get it? Did you ever think of that? That's not too far to walk, is it? That's something you could have done with the children, while I was gone. Then we wouldn't be in this fix."

"The stream is dry, Thor!"

"How do you know?"

"It always dries up in the summer."

"Have you looked at it *this* summer?"

"I don't need to look at it!"

The stream was deep down in the woods behind the house; they rarely went there. She had not a doubt of its being dry.

"Well, you'd better think about looking at it now," he cried angrily, "because I'm not going to go to Compton's today."

It was pointless, hopeless to go to the stream. But suddenly she wanted to do it, to get away from him.

"You take care of the girls," she told him. He said nothing, turning back to the horse; but she knew he would do that much. She picked up the jar from the ground. It would hold about a gallon; that was the most she could be confident she could carry through the thickets and over the mossy ledges, if by some incredible chance she should find any water to fetch home.

"I want to go too, Mama," begged Vanessa.

"No, dear," she said. "I can't take you. You stay with Papa. And look after Stella." The littler one began to whimper at the thought of her departure. Aurora hurried away around the house before her resolve to go alone could be softened by her children's disappointment.

She plunged into the woods as quickly as she could. Then she oriented herself, changed direction, and found the path. It was very steep; in the springtime, indeed, it was a stream itself. The wastrel waters had cut the boggy black soil away from tree roots, exposing gray clay and speckled granite boulders. The footing was traitorous; it seemed the stones were reaching out, trying to trip her and dash the jar from her grip; she clung to her burden tightly, stepping with exaggerated care down the rough way.

It was dark under the trees; the sky showed only as a white gap above the eroded path; yet it seemed no cooler here.

When she reached the bottom of the wood, she saw the stream was quite dry. Obviously it had been so for many weeks.

She did not want to go back yet. It would be a defeat, even though this foolish idea was Thor's, not hers. He would ask her if she had gone up the stream bed and looked to see if any spring there might still be flowing. She would anticipate the question and do it.

She followed the bed east where it wound through a cover of hemlock and massive cedars. On the banks above the stream she saw several places where the water welled up in the mud season, but these were all dry now.

As she went her way, she was surprised to realize that the bed of the stream was beautiful—surprised that she was still capable of noticing its beauty. In this place, too, the waters had scrubbed the thin forest soil off the rocks, leaving the boulders in naked heaps in the bed, stained green with algae, rounded but still rough, lumps of granite packed in place by gravity to thwart the thieving stream. The stones seemed a kind of beggar's fortune, varied as the jewels of a treasure trove, yet common and worthless.

She walked up the dry bed, ducking under bridges made by fallen arborvitae, winding her way through thickets of spruce, under the dark roofs of the fir. At length she reached a spot where the bed disappeared altogether in a broad bog that was now covered with crisp lichen and shrunken mosses. Water had been here; water would be here again; but there was no water now. Overhead the sky was silver, low, promising a change, but not affording it.

And here, at the end of the dry stream bed, she came to a halt, sinking to the ground, staring upwards through the crowded branches at a relief that refused to descend.

*My life*, she thought.

# Crossing the River

"'Why not?'—that was what you said," laughed Evert.

"I did not," protested his wife, Dorothea, laughing too—but then she became less certain. "Did I? Maybe you're right."

"And I puzzled over that 'Why not?' for four days. 'What did she mean, "Why not?"' I kept asking myself. 'Did she mean "Why wouldn't I go dancing with a fine man like you," or did she mean, "Well, no one better asked me, so you might as well be the one to take me"?' I couldn't figure it."

"You know perfectly well what I meant. I meant 'Why on earth wouldn't I go dancing with the very man I'd been pining for?'"

"I know that now," agreed Evert. "But I didn't know that then." He winked at his brother-in-law, Steen, who sat with them at the kitchen table, listening to their mutual teasing with an indulgent smile. "Let that be a lesson to you, Steen. If a woman ever says, 'Why not?', what she means is, 'What took you so long?'"

"Steen's likely to hear that a lot," said Dorothea.

"If he ever gets around to asking anyone. You'd better hurry up, Steen. You're getting older, same as the rest of us."

Steen reddened.

"I'm doing just fine," he said.

There was a brief silence, warmed by the affection of husband and wife, who were still smiling at each other over the breakfast dishes.

"Better get along, brother," said Steen. "Long way into town."

"Yup," agreed Evert, rising from his chair. "It'll be a rough road, too, after those rains."

They went outside.

Below the dooryard the land rolled over the brow of the hill and fell quickly to the river. The road led straight down to the bridge, which crossed, at a height of some dozen feet, a broad floor of red granite boulders and ledges, among which the swollen river now surged.

"I'll get the horses in, Steen," said Evert. "You take the time to chat with Dorothy. It'll probably be too long before we see you again out here."

Steen made a motion as though he felt he should really follow and help; but Dorothea caught his arm.

"You stay here," she laughed.

Evert went off to the barn, whistling contentedly.

Brother and sister looked at each other with that comfortable air that comes from long familiarity and shared memories.

"Glad to see you and Evert so happy," said Steen.

She smiled. "Oh, we are," she said. "I'll never regret marrying him. He's a good man—he's the best. I could never find another like him in the whole world."

"Only one thing bothers me," said Steen.

"What's that?"

"You're looking a little pale. A little tired."

Her expression showed some pain. "I am," she said. She looked around to make sure Evert could not hear her, and lowered her voice cautiously. "I don't sleep much at night," she said. "I can't help it. He snores, Steen."

Steen chuckled. "I know," he said. "I've heard him."

"It's not funny. I wish it were. It's his only flaw. I feel it shouldn't bother me, but it just does. I can't get by it. I've prayed for the strength to just forget it, but I can't." Now that she had begun to speak, her feelings tumbled out in angry words. Steen was amazed at the frustration that lived in her alongside her happiness. "Sometimes I think it's going to drive me mad," she said. "Yesterday I fell asleep standing up, leaning on a broom. But there's nothing I can do. I tell him to turn over, but that doesn't last. Sometimes it hardly makes a difference."

He said nothing, being at a loss for any suggestions.

She shook her head, as if deciding not to dwell on her problem anymore.

"How about you?" she asked. "You seem lonely to me, Steen. I thought when you moved up to Farr you'd meet more people. Isn't there anyone?"

He shook his head; but something in the way he did it made her press him.

"Nobody? Nobody at all?"

"Well," he said, "Maybe."

"Have you spoken to her yet?"

"I've been introduced."

"Have you asked her out?"

"No."

"Well, do it! Remember Evert and me. I waited half a year for him to get up his courage. And we were married three weeks later, and we always talk about those wasted six months."

"I don't know," he said; and then, echoing her words: "I just can't get by it."

She did not notice the allusion; or if she did, she thought it irrelevant. "Well," she said earnestly, "Pray—and do it."

He smiled at her.

"You're hopeless!" she exclaimed. "You really are!"

In a few minutes they were off. Dorothea followed the wagon to the gate, calling last-minute commissions to Evert, who promised to remember them all with the air of a man too intent on the miles before him to give heed to anybody. Steen pulled a pencil stub out of his pocket and wrote what he could on the seat of the wagon as they inched down the hill, the heavy iron-bound brake squealing.

"How are your horses on the bridge?" asked Steen.

"Oh, they don't like it any better or worse than any other horses."

"Why don't I get out and lead them through?"

"Better would be to ride Winedark. That's what I've done before."

It occurred to Steen that it would be still better if Evert did the riding, but he said nothing. At the beginning of the bridge he took his place on horseback. The horses showed no skittishness; they seemed unaware of the whirling brown water below.

Halfway across, as they were crossing the deepest, swiftest part of the river, Steen heard a tremendous crack behind him. He turned about instantly. The wagon had broken through the flooring planks on the downstream side of the bridge; already it was toppling sideways through the railing. Evert was clinging to the reins; his face was written over with fear, incomprehension, shock; and then he was gone—the falling wagon gave an irresistible tug—and the horses were dragged backwards on top of the wagon, and Steen with them.

He heard a shout, perhaps his own; and a scream, perhaps one of the horses. Then up was down; down was up; air was water; water, air. He was underwater in a tangle of harness and panicking horseflesh, kicking, even as the horses were kicking, to get free, to get to the surface.

He was swept into something inexorably hard, but had the wit to cling to it; in a moment he felt the horses pulled away from him. He clawed upwards along the obstruction and came almost immediately to the surface.

He was holding onto an abandoned stone piling downstream from the bridge. The wagon was floating, upside-down, in the stream of the current; as he watched, fighting for breath, it ran aground on a rock. The horses were upright, their frantic eyes staring wildly about as they lifted their flaring nostrils out of the foam and water; still fastened in their harness, they struggled ineffectually against the weight of the wagon and the pulse of the river.

Of Evert there was no sign. Steen thought with horror that he might be under the wagon, trapped, or crushed against the rock. He let go at once and began to swim determinedly across the current.

The river was too swift; he saw he would either miss the wagon entirely or be thrown against the horses again; he slackened his stroke just for a moment, and in that instant was whirled by the wreck. But a broad back rose under his hand from the roiling depths of the waters, and he gripped Evert by the shirt and praised God.

Almost at once they ran up on a strand of slippery boulders. Steen managed to rise and draw Evert after him; to his joy he realized his brother-in-law was moving intelligently to help him. They staggered and slid over the treacherous shoal and crawled up together on a long ledge that thrust out of the river like an island.

"Are you all right?" demanded Steen when he could get enough wind.

"The horses!" exclaimed Evert.

"Are you all right, man? Forget the horses for now!"

"Yes, yes, I'm all right. You, Steen?"

"Yes, all right. So far as I know."

He stood up on the rock, dizzily, and looked toward shore. A figure in white was standing on the bank, her hands over her heart. He waved both his hands over his head and called a reassurance that the tumult of the river muffled. "Wave, Evert," he said. "Wave, so she knows you're all right!"

Evert propped himself up groggily on one elbow and waved blindly, looking about for Dorothea. "I'm all right," he said, unable to speak more than hoarsely. On the shore Dorothea fell on her knees and clasped her hands before her.

Steen surveyed the river behind them. The rock on which the wagon had been cast was joined to their own ledge by a shallow spit of rock. He could reach the wreck in relative safety and cut the horses loose; they would have better luck swimming in the current than being slowly battered to death, trapped in their traces.

No sooner had he thought this than he was moving. He reached the wagon readily; but when he had gone that far he saw that in order to cut any key part of the harness he had to crawl out on the shivered boards and partially enter the water.

He did not want to do it. He was frightened, remembering how horrible it had been to be trapped with those animals under the muddy water; but when he realized that he was frightened, he made himself do what had to be done, against his own better sense.

He drew his clasp knife out of the pocket of his sodden trousers, set it in his teeth, and crept out along the heaving wreckage of the wagon. It seemed that at any moment the current would shoulder the wagon off the rock.

When he was about to enter the water he saw that to do so was pointless; the hind legs of the horses were thrashing and churning in the place he must descend—it would be death to do it. But he saw that he could pull out the pin that held the pole to the wagon, and let them go in their traces; and this he undertook to do. They would not stand the same chance of survival thus yoked, but any chance was an improvement.

As he pried the pin free with his knife, he felt something tighten around his ankle. Too late he realized that the reins had become wound around his boot as he had clambered about on the wreckage to get a vantage on the pin.

So when the horses surged free, they took him too. He went under, lost the knife, could not break to the surface again, felt rocks thudding into him, each one an explosion of pain. He bent double and tore at the reins wrapped around his boot.

*The boot!* he thought. He wrenched it off.

In another minute Dorothea was helping him drag himself out of the river a hundred yards downstream. "Dear God!" she kept exclaiming, in a tone of anguish, "Dear God! Dear God!"

After Dorothea ran to the neighbors with word of Evert's plight, a dozen good men came down to the river from all along the valley and found a way to pull him off the island safely. Steen was of little use but to watch and give advice; he was very bruised, and felt breathless most of the rest of the day. Some neighbors went along the bank and found the horses; they were in a shallows about a mile down. Winedark had a hideously shattered leg and was virtually lifeless; but the other horse lived, though badly beaten by the rocks.

As for Evert, he was quite hale again by the next day, and at once planned how they would finish their trip to Farr, by going on horseback well up river, where the stream was gentler and they could ford it without danger. Steen fell in with the idea, as he had to get home one way or another; and though Dorothea vetoed the plan for two days, once it was obvious they were both all right she had only vague fears with which to oppose their going.

On another early morning, then, they prepared to set out. Steen was holding the saddled horses; Evert was inside, looking for the list Dorothea had made, which he had misplaced.

"Take care as you go, Steen," said Dorothea; and it was no commonplace adieu.

"I will, don't worry," he said. "And don't worry about him," he said with a smile, knowing what her thoughts were. "I'll keep him out of trouble."

She smiled painfully.

"For all this, you know," he said, "for all the trouble you've been through in the past few days, you look better to me now than you did when I got here. You sleeping better?"

She reddened a little.

"Yes," she admitted. "When I saw the wagon fall in the river, I prayed to God that if I could only have Evert back, I'd never mind his snoring again."

"And did you mind it?"

"Not a bit. The first night I woke up when he started, but I just snuggled closer and thought how lucky I was. And you know, I haven't heard him snoring since. For all I know, he's stopped altogether."

"Oh, no," said Steen. "He hasn't stopped. I can tell you that. I went out to sleep in the barn last night to get away from it."

Evert, coming out of the house just then, wondered what private joke they were grinning at; but knew better than to ask.

Two days later they were in Farr. Evert had to buy various tools, some seed, and a long list of Dorothea's commissions, including cloth, needles, and thread. In particular he wanted a color of thread to match a sample she had given him. He could not find it; and after he had tried without success at two shops, he proclaimed it would be the ruin of his marriage if he came home without it, and threw himself on Steen's greater knowledge of the town.

Steen took him to a dry goods store that looked out over the lake harbor. "How do you know about this place?" asked Evert. "I never knew this was here."

"I live in this town, remember?"

Evert humphed, as if that were not sufficient explanation. While he went to the counter, Steen hung back, studying the set of the teeth on a bucksaw hanging on the wall. In a minute Steen heard Evert say, "Where's Steen? Steen! Come look at these two threads and tell me which matches better."

Steen went slowly to the counter, his eyes on the floor.

Evert showed him the spools. "Hard to tell," said Steen. "What do you think?" he asked the woman behind the counter, raising his eyes to hers with difficulty.

"This one," she said.

"That's what I would have said, too," mumbled Steen.

"You didn't even look which one she pointed to," said Evert. "What's come over you, Steen?—Here, Miss, I'll take this. I trust your judgment. But heaven help me if you're wrong."

"You could always buy both," she suggested quietly.

Evert laughed and pushed both spools toward her. "This girl's sharp, ain't she, Steen?"

Steen muttered something incoherent. He went outside while Evert completed the purchase.

In another hour Evert had packed his new goods on the horse and gone. He said he could make a few miles before sundown, and he would sleep better knowing he was a few miles closer to Dorothea. Steen watched him ride off with regret, already lonely, and envying him that sense of purpose that comes from having a companion waiting at home.

He wandered about the town for a while, loath to go home himself. The sun was westering over the lake; he went down to the water and watched it.

*How different the lake water is,* he thought. *But still, it's cold and dark, and you can't breathe in it.*

He looked into the depths of the lake and thought about how a few days ago he had almost died, almost been killed crossing the river.

Suddenly he started away from the lakeside. He went back up along the shore, to where the dry goods store looked out over the harbor.

Inside he quailed as suddenly as he had made his resolution just a few moments before. He studied the saw again. Several customers left the store; the place was empty except for the woman at the counter.

*You were almost dead a few days ago,* he said to himself. *You might be dead a few days from now. Why not do it?*

He forced himself to turn, and went up to the counter, walking with a wooden stride.

He looked her directly in the face. She looked evenly back at him. Neither of them spoke.

"Miss Dunellen," he said finally.

"Yes, Mr. Steen?"

"How are you?"

"Well, thank you. And you? You've been out of town for a while, I hear."

He forgot to answer. He took a deep breath, bracing himself.

"What I wanted to know—Fridays usually there's a dance over at the meeting hall—"

But he could say no more. After a moment more of silence, he appealed to her with his eyes.

She smiled, rubbing her thumb with telltale nervousness back and forth along the counter.

"Why not?" she said.

# The Indweller

Once on a time there was a woman who was possessed by an evil spirit.

Perhaps the ill would have stopped there, but that she was the wife of a man; and so the evil spirit not only tormented her, but it brought him grief that was, perhaps, even worse than the pain she suffered.

Her name was Hunnikin. The man, whose name was Kort, called her "Hunni," of course; and well she deserved the name.

Her voice was soft; she spoke with a kind of abstraction that made her seem—or revealed that she was—often distant among other thoughts, better thoughts than the world at large had need of. When she began to speak, her words drifted forth from her being like flakes of snow falling into a tepid pool in which they instantly dissolved.

She was wise in many things. Although often her handiwork faltered, due to her concentration upon other matters, the man did not fault her for it; for she was a mate to his mind, sharing many of his thoughts, both those that were simple and those that were complected with all the contradictory strains of his being.

Then, too, she was beautiful. To tell a woman's beauty is a task outworn by the ages; but it needs to be said that she was upright, slim-waisted, with an abundance of golden brown hair and with eyes of a handsome blue. Her hands and her feet were perhaps the most telling features of her beauty: for they were neither too large nor too small, but crafted in fairness and proportion, fit for their tasks, and yet fit as well to be admired. Her husband liked well to take her into his lap, and, with one arm about her, to hold her hands or grip her feet while they talked of this or another matter.

He liked as well when the time came for bed, when the day was over, and the work done; when the fire was banked up for the night, the great thick doors of the house bolted fast, and the little one tucked away snug under a goose-feather quilt. If he could, he would make himself ready before his wife did, so that he could be sitting in bed watching when she took off her clothes, for he dearly enjoyed that—how her back arched as she drew the blouse off over her head, and her fair fine breasts stood forth, startled by the sudden chill. And when she lay beside him, he would draw the hem of the nightdress up to her waist, and run his fingers through the dark hair where her thighs met her belly, and kiss her on her smiling mouth, until her loving smile grew slack, and her eyelids slipped partway closed, and she joined him in delight.

Her love for her husband was of that kind that demonstrates why God made humankind in the first place, and why It permits the race to continue to exist, despite all human sins and crimes. She loved him bravely, tenaciously, hopefully; for though in his way he was a good man, he had many foibles and made many false starts on his way after happiness. In short, he was human, and she loved him in spite of that, even because of that; and that was what made her love noble, that it was forgiving, that it overrode all the obstructions that his own person and behavior constantly offered to it, and loved him anyway.

He, for his part, loved her likewise; although in Hunni herself there was less to be forgiven than there was in him. He could happily have loved her to the end of his days, without ever a cross word to her, without ever raising his voice, or stalking out of the house; cherishing her in kindness—content, despite all poverty and hardship and crossed dreams, with her quiet presence.

But as it was, he had not so easy a time of it. For be Hunni what she was, there was that evil spirit that had taken up its lodgings in her; and that was what made him struggle against anger and resentment day after day.

He had not known of the bad spirit for many years. His ignorance of it had made loving his wife much harder; for he had not been able to untangle the good from the bad—he had been hurt so often that at last he had come to be suspicious even of the good in her; and he had come finally to think it incredible when she embraced him, or spoke soft words to him, or told him she loved him, since her fair speech was so at odds with the work of the evil spirit in her.

Then one winter morning, when his wife was away, many days' journey over the hills visiting her people, he lay in bed until a little after dawn, half awake and half asleep, listening to a rain that was falling on the roof of the house; and in the rain, like a kind of whisper, he heard the truth about his wife. They say that when the angels choose to speak, they do so with the voices of the wind and the rain, so perhaps it was some angel who at last took pity on these two suffering people and whispered the truth to him.

"Hunni is possessed," the rain seemed to say. "An indweller lives in her—an evil spirit named Mara. A wizard persecuted and pursued her once, and she took up refuge in Hunni long before you ever met her. Now Mara is trapped inside her. But she has come to like her abode; every day she grows more used to it; every day she thrusts Hunni more and more into a corner and takes over a little more. She has come to need you—to thrive upon your affection for Hunni, and on her own irrepressible will to torment you. You must learn to see what in the woman is Hunni and what is Mara, so that you can love Hunni still, and help her hold Mara aside."

When the man heard this, he jumped out of the bed with a cry; for he knew instantly that it was true, and it explained both his hurt and his love for his wife.

When his moment of relief and exultation had ended, he called upon the rain to tell him what he must do to exorcise this spirit Mara. But the rain was again only rain; the angel, if angel it had been, had withdrawn.

Though Kort was disappointed in the silence, he was still grateful for what he had learned.

He soon came to distinguish Mara's evil work from Hunni's goodness. For instance, his wife frequently told him that he alone of all those she had known truly cared for her and listened to her. Before he had heard the speech of the rain, he had always received this in silence, with much inward bitterness; for it had often seemed his wife did not care for his interests or listen to him for more than the time it took to satisfy an idle curiosity. But he saw now that it was Mara who prevented Hunni from listening to him. Hunni cared deeply for him; she would have heard him out and taken an interest in his cares and in his pleasures, however odd they might be. (And even he would have admitted that they were often strange.) But Mara was not the least bit interested in these matters.

There was one part of their life together where Mara's influence was growing weaker. That was when Kort and Hunni met together in bed for the loving of their flesh. In the early years, Mara had commanded here, too. She had felt Kort's love for the body in which she dwelt as a danger, an intrusion; she seldom would permit him to touch her in any way that suggested his desire for her, and dreary weeks would drag by in which she turned away coldly from him, without a kiss, without a goodnight, without any sign that she knew or cared that he existed.

But as the marriage had grown in years, Hunni had asserted herself more. For her, tenderness was a sweet spring, always running over, both waking and slaking thirst. Mara then would find that she was swept along with Hunni's affection; and as time passed, she grew to crave the pleasure she felt in watching Hunni and Kort joining in love, even while she feared and hated it. Here he had hope, for if Hunni could come to the fore in this, might she not also succeed in other matters as well, where now Mara still held sway exclusively?

Before he had heard the voice of the rain, his hope had been much reduced. He contemplated the future and saw only pain; for he was so miserable under the fractious torments of Mara that he knew he could not live out the rest of his life with his wife; and yet he deeply loved Hunni, and he did not know how to live without her. And then too there was the little one, who was a strong bond between them, a bond that not even Mara could destroy. Thus there was pain before him, whether he stayed with her, or whether he left her.

Now he thought he might, after all, find a way out of his torture without hurting Hunni or himself. That way, it seemed, was to show Hunni that Mara dwelt in her; for he thought that if she had seen Mara within her, she might be able to combat and defeat her other self, even if she could not drive her out completely.

He prayed for help.

No answer came. Things went on as they had; Mara grew stronger; and though Hunni struggled with her, her resistance had little effect.

Then one day Kort was out walking on the land, and a bold wind was blowing overhead. It was March, and all the earth was beginning to listen to the fine, high piping hidden in the air, the warmth that said, Come alive; hope.

And Kort remembered hearing once that a mirror could catch an evil spirit. If the one possessed looked into a mirror, she would see the indweller; and if she then broke the glass, the spirit would be slain.

As he remembered this he thought he heard a voice again, in the wind. And this time it said: "Don't tamper with God's will, Kort. Don't try to shrug off before its term the suffering that God has set on your shoulders."

*Is it God's will that I should suffer?* he thought. *Or that Hunni should suffer?* And it seemed to him that the answer to these questions was no.

He turned about on his heel and hastened home. When he strode into the house again, Mara bickered at him—she was now suspicious of his every move, for she had sensed that he had detected her. But he only kissed Hunni kindly on the mouth, and went to his workshop.

Of mirrors he knew little, but he learned. He taught himself the making of glass, its pouring and cooling, the silver laid down upon it; he made with his old skill the frame of wood and bound the mirror in it. And somewhere, he felt, at some point in the process of his craftsmanship, he bound into the mirror the magic of his love. He was not sure he was doing so; indeed, when he was finished with it, he doubted that the mirror was anything extraordinary; but all the same, perhaps the power lay hidden in the glass, waiting for its time to speak.

He chose an hour when they would be alone. Quiet was in the house; the window of the room downstairs stood open, and a dreaming breeze blew in, to which Hunni hearkened as if she, too, could hear it speaking; but it was only the abstraction that took her, the absentness so dear to him.

"I've made you something," he said, holding the mirror behind his back. She looked up.

For a moment there was a struggle, and some doubt. At first Hunni smiled, but then Mara frowned; and the upshot was silence. He winced inwardly. No matter how well he prepared himself for the pain, it hurt no less.

"So that's what you've been working on," she said, hurtfully and carelessly vague.

He brought the mirror and sat down on a stool before her. The looking glass was small but heavy; he held it out in his two hands and she looked into it.

She started. Then she let out a low shriek and fell forward in a faint, dashing her head against the mirror so sharply that the glass cracked.

"Hunni!" he cried. He drew the broken mirror away from her and cast it aside, catching up his wife in his arms and crying her name again and again.

The woman he held came back to consciousness; he felt the quickening in her limbs.

"Hunni?" she repeated. Then, in a harsh voice: "Gone, and good riddance to her."

Kort pushed her away in horror and stared; for the voice was the voice of Mara. And the eyes, too, that glared back at him, were the hard, hateful eyes of the wrong woman.

# Archon's Gift

For E.W.P.

Clement could not have said when the yearning began. Perhaps it was in the summer. At that time of year he ate his supper on the porch, sitting upright in a straight-backed chair, dead-center before the steps, watching the sun as it turned downwards under the hills. He stayed where he was for a long time on those evenings, as the sky caught quiet fire. He was too tired to move; he knew he should go to bed, to rise reknit for another day's fraying; but he was too tired, and besides, he could not give himself up to sleep so soon. It was too much like death. Not so soon, not when the sky was aflame; not until the fire fell to a glow and then was quenched in coal. His plans, his schemes for breaking the hold of the poverty that had bound him all his life, even they lost their attraction, seeming bitterly and utterly impossible of fruition.

These were the times he had the yearning. He felt lonely; he even felt hungry; his hands felt restless on his knees; and his ear sought with a kind of pining wonder after each distant sound on the farm, one after another, as if testing them, while a voice in him said *No, that's not it; no, that's not it.*

Then one day, after about a year of wondering, it came to him what he wanted. He wanted to play music.

He had never played music; he had never known how. Once, when he was a boy, he had had a guitar for a time, and had taught himself a few songs on it; but the strings had broken, and he had not been able to buy new ones immediately; and before he could, the guitar had been broken somehow, he could not recall quite how.

He thought he would like to do that—have a guitar and try to play music. He was starting too late to ever really be good at it; but no one else had to listen to it. As long as it pleased him, that was all that mattered.

Many months passed after he identified the yearning. He was by now quite sure he was right about it; but he had done nothing towards fulfilling his wish. A guitar would cost money, and he had none to spare. Every time he sat down to his reckoning, he saw his hope of coaxing a little spare cash out of his funds disappear in the need for a new shoeing for the mule or for those seed potatoes to replace the crop the blight had taken last year.

Then, just as autumn was turning its gray face toward the white winter, he had occasion to go up to Farr. He had word his sister was ill, like to die; but by the time he arrived there, she was so much out of danger that she was sorry to have put him to the trouble.

Since he was in town he went the rounds of the shops; and in one he found not just a single guitar but three, hanging from a beam in a dark corner that smelled of balsam and crisp calico and cold iron nails. A fellow saw him eyeing them.

"Take one down and try it out," he said briskly.

Clement mumbled something.

"Here," the fellow said. He took a guitar from its pegs, tuned it expertly, and jangled off a quick melody. Then he thrust it at Clement. "Try it," he said. "Go on."

Clement would not touch it. He felt embarrassed because he hardly even knew how to hold it. "How much?" he asked. The man named a price—high, but not utterly out of Clement's reach.

"Let me think about it," he said.

"Sure thing," said the fellow, shrugging. He hung the guitar back on the beam.

Clement went away and thought about it. He knew he could borrow the money from his sister—she was particularly grateful to him now for the concern he had shown in hurrying to see her in her illness—and he could pay her back soon, perhaps, if he could make his traps pay off.

But second thoughts proved louder than his yearning. Maybe it was prudence, or maybe it was that at heart, he did not believe in being good to himself. He did go back to the shop, and stared at the guitar for a while; but the fellow who had been so forthright before was not about. So he left, and the opportunity passed.

On his road home he met an old friend. Clement and Archon had not seen each other for ten years, and the miles, though cold and autumn-wet, were briefly passed, and soon they came to where the road forked to Archon's.

"Come down to the house," he said. "It's just a half-hour out of your way. I'll put you up and send you off with a full belly and dry boots tomorrow." Clement was persuaded, and followed Archon home.

The place was small and a bit ramshackle, but snug enough. They lit a fire and sat before it as they ate their supper. The wind sucked thirstily at the chimney top, puffing up the flames as effectively as a bellows. In that pale glow the two men talked over old times and present perplexities.

They were both poor. Fifty years of working on the land had brought no cessation; but though Clement was still struggling after that elusive ease, Archon could laugh at his ambition. "You were always for getting rich," said Archon with a soft smile.

"I've tried about everything," remembered Clement, ruefully. "First I was going to do it on wheat. I plowed up every square inch of my forty acres. I even had wheat growing in the dooryard."

"What happened?" asked Archon, trying to recall.

"Rust took it."

"That's right."

"Then there was timber; those big oaks, remember? Fellow wanted them for bell frames in big churches. But they were all shot through with ants."

"The oaks," said Archon, nodding.

"Then there was corn meal. I was going to get a corner on the market, grind it in my own mill."

"What ever made you think of getting rich on corn meal?" chuckled Archon. They ruminated for a while, until finally Archon spoke again. "I guess I always knew I was going to be poor. Right from the start."

"Remember that time we got drunk?" said Clement. "Must have been when we were about twenty. You told me that all you really wanted in life was to travel around, playing your fiddle; but you thought you'd starve to death, or be driven from town to town. I told you that when I was rich, I'd give you the money to do it. You named what you needed—it wasn't much, I remember. I was sure I was going to get rich and have the money to spare. I know I promised you'd have the first of my money if ever I got any."

"I remember," said Archon, smiling. "Which is pretty amazing, because I was pretty drunk at the time."

Clement stared into the fire.

"I still wish I were rich," he said. "I could still set you up, Archon."

"Forget it," advised Archon. "I haven't been unhappy. I've sat here many an evening, all by myself, playing the fiddle, perfectly glad I wasn't crouching in some cold barn somewhere with the cows."

"You still play the fiddle?" asked Clement, almost enviously.

"Of course," said Archon.

The flames painted the walls of the small room with a hue like sunset.

And Clement, watching the slow flaring of the fire, suddenly decided to tell Archon about his yearning after music.

He was shy about it. He knew Archon had played from the time he was a boy, and had always been very good. His own desire to play might seem foolish.

But Archon listened with ready understanding. He gave advice and suggested ways in which Clement could teach himself. When he was done, the two men sat in silence for a while. Clement felt warmed and encouraged; but he thought of that guitar hanging from the beam in the shop back in Farr, and he felt no closer to what he needed. After a time, Archon snapped his fingers.

"And I've even got a guitar I could give you," he said. "It's an old one—the first one I ever had. I'm kind of attached to it, but seeing how I don't use it, I ought to give it to you. A good guitar gets dull if it isn't played."

Clement sat in mute hope, feeling any expression of his sudden delight would seem like greed.

"And I think I know where it is," said Archon, as if this were the most astonishing part of all. "You stay here. I'll go get it."

Clement waited. Archon talked to himself upstairs and down; it seemed the guitar was not where he had thought it would be, but there were other possibilities—perhaps the attic. After ten or fifteen minutes of search he found it.

Clement hardly dared look at it when he brought it down. It was too beautiful—scarred, simple, but solid. Archon chatted about it as he restrung it, tuned it, and played a few songs. Then, like the man in the shop, he turned to Clement and held it out. "There you are," he said. "Try it."

"I wouldn't dare," said Clement. "Try playing it, I mean. Not here. Not till I've had a chance to practice by myself. I won't ever be a musician, you know." He took the guitar reverently in his hands, but would not touch the strings, though he was eager to.

It was several days after he had returned home before he finally took up the guitar with the intention of playing it. He spent most of the first evening with it trying to get the tuning right, or at least as right as his uninstructed ear allowed. The next night he began plucking at it and strumming it. Archon had written down some advice and given him some sheet music, and he pored over this, trying to make sense of it. After about an hour it became clear that he was quite hopeless; he would never be a musician; his yearning was only one of the many distractions that had called him away from all he really could do, which was work the land. And even at that he had not been so lucky as to make his fortune.

He put the guitar out of his mind for several evenings. Instead he worked out the figures for a new scheme that would make him wealthy. This time it was strawberries. He was sure he could grow them, transport them to Farr, ship them on his brother-in-law's lake schooner, and sell them fresh in the city. City folks were willing to pay anything for a fresh berry.

He calculated beds and rows, numbers of plants, and studied up on strawberry cultivation; he wrote to a man he knew who had good stock; and he determined that in about three years he could get his investment paid off and start seeing a good return. It would be a lot of work. Nothing choked a strawberry faster than the kind of weeds he had around here; and he had slugs in the garden, too, that would scar a berry and make it look pretty unappetizing to fastidious city folk.

The idea grew on him, more strongly than any of his other plans had. He was convinced this would be the one that would work. And as he dreamed of the rewards, a large part of his satisfaction lay in the thought of being able to go to Archon and give him some money, if he would take it.

Because even if Clement was almost frightened of that guitar, he deeply felt Archon's generosity.

Despite his despair of ever being a musician, about a week after he had settled on the strawberry scheme,

Clement found himself with the guitar in his hands again. He could not resist. He thought that even if he could not make sense of the strings, he might still pluck something pleasing out of them.

And so, without knowing what he was doing, Clement gradually began to play. At first he picked tunes out of the guitar almost at random, unable to repeat them, even when they haunted him. But as winter came on, and set in, and passed away, he found he could set his hands to the instrument and play, in one manner or other, just about any tune he could bring to his lips. The comments Archon had scratched out for him now began to make sense. Sometimes his music sounded thin, and he knew he needed schooling in the chords; but it pleased him all the same.

He would think about that pleasure the moment he woke. Even if the day was to be all chores and hard tasks—the hauling of cordwood and the long march over the drifted hills after his traps, the endless scraping and stretching of pelts—still he could think of that moment after supper when he took up the guitar and lost himself in the satisfaction of his own music. Sometimes he fell asleep over the instrument, loath to give it up.

And the more pleasure he won out of the guitar, the more he thought with gratitude of Archon. His friend had made this possible. He had shared music with Clement without hesitation.

Music, Clement thought, was as boundless as friendship itself—the more of yourself you gave to it, the more you found in yourself to give.

As spring neared, Clement received his answer about the strawberry stock. He took his savings from the traps and went over to Brixton one day in mud season; the stock looked good, and he bought as much as he could afford.

With the new season suddenly he had too much to do. A whole day passed without his being able to play the guitar, and he woke the next morning grim and angry and weary of life, because he knew he would again be too busy for music. And all this was before he began work on the strawberry beds. First he had to get his usual garden in. His plow broke; the mule went lame; the rains washed out the beans, and the crows got to them; then the season went dry and the garden started to outright blow away; then a late frost stung his seedlings. It was two weeks into blackfly season before he could even think about the strawberry stock, which by now was looking half-rotten.

He had promised himself one evening with the guitar before he took on the berry beds. Exhausted and cheerless, he turned to the instrument almost desperately; and as he had known it would, it healed him of his weariness and bitterness, teaching him how bored he had been listening to the emptiness of his own thoughts day after day.

He had set his chair out on the porch. The night was chilly and the flies were gone, lying in the long grass out of the wind. He played until he had played enough; until the sun had sunken and utterly vanished, and the stars had started out in pinprick relief against the black sky.

*Tomorrow,* he thought, *I'll start the strawberries. And if I can make that work, I swear I'll give the first profits to Archon.*

The thought of the dreary work before him dampened his smile.

*And so what?* he thought. *What would the money mean to him? He gave me music; all I could give him would be cash.*

True generosity, he realized, consists of giving not what you wish you had, but what you really do have. All his dreams of helping Archon with money had only undermined his ability to show his gratitude for what his friend had done.

The stars spun by degrees around the Pole Star, while Clement sat on the porch, growing colder, growing older, thinking about the striving after wealth that had tortured and driven him all these years—a torment that he had ordained for himself tomorrow, and the next day, and the next, until the day he died.

*It isn't worth it,* he decided finally. *The digging, the setting, the weeding, hauling the berries down to Farr, so rich people can pay too much for them. I'd rather sit here on this porch and play this guitar than break my back trying to be the richest man in the whole county. I'd rather play this guitar than* be *the richest man in the county, come to think of it, even if I could get rich by snapping my fingers. Let the strawberries rot!*

He grinned.

What would he do tomorrow, then? The crops were in; he had a few days to spend on whatever he wanted. One thing he would do was play his guitar—go up the hill where it was windy, out of the flies, and just play as much as he wanted. Another thing he would do would be to decide some way to show Archon how grateful he was.

But what could that be? What would mean as much to Archon as Archon's gift had meant to Clement?

*I'll go play for him,* thought Clement. *Then he'll know how glad I am. I'll bet he'll be pretty surprised at how well I've done, all by myself.*

He laughed softly. *Maybe he'll get out his fiddle and play with me,* he thought. *Then we'll be the two richest poor men on Earth.*

# Who Holds Thee?



Kalander had known Strephon and Alyss for eighteen years—eighteen years of mutual labor and friendship.

He had helped them build their house. When they could not find on their own land a tree straight enough and thick enough to be the roofbeam of the house they were raising, he had offered one of his own. Alyss called it "Kalander's timber," and Strephon had carved a *K* in it. People told Kalander how they had seen that letter, as they sat by the fire and tilted back in the rocking chair, looking into the golden shadows of the high ceiling spaces; and how Strephon had told the story of it with pride and affection.

Kalander and Strephon plowed and sowed and mowed together. In the winter they cut wood and sledged it down the hills with Kalander's great workhorses. Strephon brought, unasked, of his own remembering, a wagon of manure from his cows for Kalander's kitchen garden every year, because it was better for herbs and vegetables than horse manure. When they sat together over dinner, which was as often as once a week, they traded accounts of how the corn was growing, and what to do about that old woodchuck under the common pasture wall, and the other vital gossip of farm life. At the harvest celebration they set up a ring and had a wrestle, for they were both wrestlers from childhood; they pretty much traded victories from year to year. And at every season of they year, they laughed a good deal; for Strephon and Alyss had a good sense of humor, which Kalander appreciated.

Strephon and Alyss had great respect for Kalander. Not only had he a good hand with a rein and an axe, a plane and a hoe, but he was a very well-read man, self-taught. He knew Greek; and sometimes he would read to the children, translating as he went, strange tales of one-eyed monsters and kings come home from long-ago wars. Two dozen books, bound in faded leather, leaned comfortably together on a stout board on the wall near his chimney corner—more books, Strephon said, than any other library this side of Farr.

Kalander was a widower. It was a mark of Alyss's familiarity with him that she could tease him about finding a wife to help him; but when she did, he always said he never thought of it. No one knew whether it was because he had been happy with his wife, or miserable; but folks thought it was probably the latter. "When I come here, I see all of marriage I need to see," he used to say to Alyss ambiguously, by way of turning her teasing on her. She would laugh, and like as not chase the children away to give him a little more peace, saying, "We don't want to give the wedded state a bad name, then."

He liked all their children well. First was Miranda; then the two boys, Strephie and Turner, and then the littlest girl, Genevra, who was but five. Of these Miranda was the most remarkable. She had been born soon after the house had been raised. Kalander often told Miranda how he had come back to the stead-ing after fetching the midwife and seen her already in Strephon's arms, a wee mewling bit of a thing no bigger than a butternut squash.

In fact, Kalander had given her her name. Strephon had asked what they should call this wonder of a girl; and Kalander had said, "Miranda"; saying it meant "She who should be wondered at." Strephon always thought the name was Greek, though when Miranda grew old enough she told him he was wrong.

Miranda was a smart one. She ate up every book the schoolmistress had; she stripped every fact out of old Mistress Furthright's head and left it about bare of anything but amazement at that "wonderful girl who never got done learning." There was no feeding such an intellect with what could be found on the farm; at fourteen she went off to live with her aunt, where better schooling could be had. She came back often, of course—holidays and summers; to quarrel with her mother, and complain that her brothers were unbearable, to forget her chores, to giggle with her girlfriends, to prattle her scorn of boys—in short, to dutifully perform the business of growing up.

She asked Kalander to teach her Greek. He promised he would; but between the hoeing and the harvest, between his mending wall and tending his horses, and all his other tasks, he never found the time; or if he did, she was off square dancing or picnicking.

During her last year at her aunt's, she wrote a post-script to a long letter home: "Tell Kalander I've been learning Greek." Kalander smiled when they showed him this. He had just stepped in for a minute on a dark January night; now he leaned back in the rocking chair and a soft look came over his features, as if he were remembering when his eyes first opened in that language. "I'm glad for her," he said. "It'll be a whole new world to her."

"But what will she do with it?" wondered Alyss, folding the letter up and tucking it back into her basket of knitting. "This is her world, here, for better or worse. She's coming home in June to stay this time. She doesn't want to teach school; she never has. What will she do with a head full of Greek and who knows what else? She'll be too good for her chores."

"Oh, aye," said Kalander drily. "Greek spoils a body for any use. Don't you agree, Strephon?"

Husband and wife laughed. "You know I don't mean you," said Alyss. "But who will have her?"

"More important," said Strephon, "Who will she have? I thought she used to like that Jerrit boy; but last Christmas she said he was too stupid." He set another log on the fire and then shook his head fondly. "She keeps going on like this, she'll make us all look stupid," he added.

"She'll find her way," said Kalander. And then he added, with a kindly wink: "The body calls louder than the brain."

One morning in late June Kalander went out to weed his potatoes. He started at dawn, knowing that in the cool of the day he would avoid the black flies; but when the sun grew hot, he still kept on, for once he started anything, it was hard for him to stop. Finally the flies won. He ran back up to the house, washed his face and neck in cool water, and brushed the flies out of his beard. Then he thought how he was fiercely hungry, and went to the cupboard where he kept his bread.

He was interrupted by a faint knock on the door post. Miranda was standing in the doorway, smiling at him. In her hand was a basket. "Caught you just in time," she said. "Mama said you'd be out fighting the flies. Wouldn't have any breakfast, and then just when you were good and miserable, you'd sprint for the house."

"Well, I guess she knows me," said Kalander. "When did you get home? I knew you were coming soon, but I hadn't heard when."

"Yesterday. I've brought you your dinner, Kalander." On her face was a smile, secret and nervous and eager.

"Have you!" exclaimed Kalander. He found preparing even a simple meal a dreary task.

"It was Mama's idea. I told her I wanted to read Greek with you, and she said the only way I'd ever catch you sitting still was to take you your dinner every day and make you listen to me while you ate."

He laughed. "Open your basket, girl. What do you want to read?"

"I haven't read Homer yet."

"Then you haven't read Greek."

He fetched his copy while she set the dinner out on the table. He saw with approval that she had brought thick pieces of Alyss's bread, fresh butter, a wedge of cheese, some strawberries, and a little jug of cream.

"Did I pick your favorite things?" she asked.

"I'm not a complicated man," said Kalander. "I'd be happy with just the bread and cheese."

They sat down at the table. Kalander opened the book and they leaned their heads over it together. They forgot the food.

"First line," said Kalander.

"Oh, dear," she said. "It doesn't look anything like what I've read."

He grinned. "What have you read? The Book?"

She nodded.

"Don't worry," he said. He pointed out a word with a thick, callused finger stained green by the lambsquarters he had pulled out of the potato beds.

"'Goddess,'" she said happily. Then: "'Anger.'"

"Not just 'anger,'" he said. "'Wrath.'"

"'Sing, goddess, the wrath—'"

"These are genitives."

"'Of Achilles—'"

"Son of Peleus. Now the whole line—and this, too—"

"'Accursed?'"

"Right. I like 'baneful,' myself."

She put her finger on the page and pieced the words together.

"Sing, Goddess, the baneful wrath of Achilles, son of Peleus . . ."

Kalander reached for the bread and butter.

"Keep going," he said.

All that summer she came at the noon hour. After a time he insisted she leave off bringing her parents' food. He had ample, and they had six mouths. So she made his dinner of what was in his cupboards.

He enjoyed her visits. The food tasted better when her hands had set it out; he did not know why. They sat outside, after the flies had gone in July; the light was better. Kalander would look down the long hollow where his corn and wheat and protatoes were thriving, eating heartily while she nibbled on a strawberry or later a plum or a green apple. She held the book in her lap, with her knees drawn up so high, and her head bent down so low, that sometimes he teased her that she would put her face in the pages. As for himself, he knew the old tale so well he rarely had to look at the words.

After the first week he let her take the book home to study the next day's lesson ahead. That Saturday Alyss complained that Miranda would not even go with the family to a dance. Kalander only laughed. "A Greek old maid, that's what she'll be," he said. "I heard tell of one, once."

"I hardly think it's a joke," said Alyss, in a tone more bitter than he had ever heard her use. "If you had a child, you'd know what I mean. Raising a girl just to see her addled!"

"I thought you encouraged her to come read with me," he said, surprised at her vehemence.

"I did," she admitted. He saw that she was torn. "She wanted to so badly, and she loves it so much. But I never thought she'd give everything else up."

"Is she keeping up with her chores?"

"Oh, yes! I've never seen her work so hard. It's like she's trying to prove something."

"Don't worry, then, Alyss. Love is in the blood. Someday she'll look up at that Jerrit boy, and it'll be the old story all over again."

"There's another old story filling up her heart right now, Kalander. It came from that book of yours. There's no room in her heart for anything else."

"She'll write a new one in on top of it. You'll see."

One day in midsummer, well before the noon hour was over, they finished the first volume. He thought she would run to fetch the second; but instead they sat in silence. She seemed to be almost in a trance; he stole glances at her from time to time; she radiated an eager and yet dreamy contentment, a complete satisfaction with the moment.

After a very long time she turned to him. Her eyes, he noticed, were hazel—clear, wide, and young. He must have known their color before, he thought; and yet he did not remember ever noticing it.

"Kalander, will you tell me something?" she asked.

"Of course."

"What was your wife like?"

"My wife? Why were you kids always so curious about my wife?"

"You never told us anything."

He shook his head.

"There isn't much to tell. Just the old story. I met her; we fell in love; we married; she died about a year afterwards. That was a long time ago. About . . . five years before you were born."

"You must have been awfully young."

"Awfully," he said drily. "About your age, in fact."

"What was she like?" Miranda persisted.

"Oh . . . she was kind. A gentle woman. A good woman."

"I knew it," she said suddenly. "Mama always used to think she was a shrew. I knew she wasn't; I knew if she had been, you would have tried again. I know you're not a quitter."

"No, I'm no quitter. Or I like to think I'm not. And she was no shrew. She was . . . just everything. When she died I knew there would be no other. I just knew it. And there hasn't been. She was my whole love story, beginning, middle, and end, in that one year. Maybe that's why I took to your folks so much. They seemed to be living out what I could have lived out with Greta."

"Could she read Greek?"

He was mildly surprised at the thought. "What, Greta? No, girl. She hardly knew to spell her own name."

Miranda turned away. She seemed to have crimsoned.

"I don't mind your asking," he said, to reassure her.

But she smiled at him, and he saw that she was not embarrassed; she seemed, rather, to be trying to control a feeling like elation.

Harvest came. Kalander and Strephon wrestled; and this year it was a drawn match.

Harvest went by. The nights were cold, but the days always warmed by the nooning. And Kalander and Miranda met still and read.

They finished the book the day before All-Hallows Eve. Miranda took it as a matter of course that they would at once go on with the next; and Kalander, although he tried to coax her into leaving off for a while, for Alyss's sake, finally brought out the book and put it into her hands.

The next day she did not come at the usual time. The day was warm; he sat on the ledge where they were accustomed to read together and waited for her. From this spot he could look down the hollow and see her approaching.

In a few minutes she appeared. He saw why she was late; she had her sister Genevra by the hand. The little girl was marching upward with a mixture of reluctance and dread, and Kalander chuckled as he guessed why.

He had built a spook-scare for All-Hallows Eve. It was a custom of his; one year he had done it to amuse the children, and then, of course, they insisted he carry on the tradition. He used the scarecrow frame, dressed in black rags, with a small pumpkin for a head, and an old, bent, rusty scythe to make it look like the Reaper himself. At night it was quite convincing. Strephie and Turner were just reaching an age to boast that it meant nothing to them; but not Genevra. She would not admit she was afraid; and she was so fascinated by it that she could not leave it alone. He had seen her stealing around the foot of the hollow several times in the past few days; and though he had called to her, she had only run away.

With Miranda's hand in hers she came halfway up the slope to the bugaboo. Then she bolted and sped off with a shriek; and Miranda's laughing reassurances were too late to instill courage in her. At last Miranda went straight up to the spookscare herself and called, "Ginny! Ginny! Look, it's just a silly old scarecrow!"

"She's long gone," said Kalander.

Miranda turned and smiled at him—young, straight, vital, the opposite of the caricature beside her.

"You're not afraid of the Reaper?" he asked jokingly.

"Not me."

"Read up on your lesson?" he asked. "Come on, I'm starving."

"I haven't had time. But I brought your dinner, and you can listen to me falter my way through the first page."

She came to the rock and set the basket down beside him. "Going to the dance tonight?" he asked.

"What dance?"

"I hear there's one over in Moschus's new barn."

She shook her head, berating his foolishness with another smile. "Why would I go to a dance when I can sit home and read Greek?"

He felt a twinge of guilt as he realized she was perfectly serious. "Well," he said, "there are generally young men at dances."

"So?"

"Well . . ." He groped for a gentle way to phrase it. "Young women generally like young men."

Her smile had become . . . he could not have said exactly what quality it had—that strange radiant contentment, sufficiency.

To his surprise, she stepped around behind him suddenly and knelt at his back. Her strong hands pressed lightly over his face, hiding his eyes.

"Guess who?" she said, in an altered voice.

Something was happening he did not understand. Instinctively he tried to joke with her.

"Youth," he said, thinking of how she had looked, standing by the spookscare.

She seemed to be hesitating, overcome by that emotion he could not identify.

"No," she whispered finally. "Not Youth, but Love."

And the strong hands let him go.

He turned around. Her hazel eyes were brimming with tears.

"What is it?" he asked, confused. "What's the matter?"

Suddenly she gripped his head again, and kissed him, lightly and yet firmly, on the lips.

"I love you, Kalander," she said.

Then she rose and ran away, before he could think, before he could call after her, before he could know what he was feeling himself.

He heard Strephon and Alyss coming up the hollow about an hour later. He went to the door and waited for them. Alyss had been crying, he saw; he thought he heard Strephon say something about letting an old friend explain.

They caught sight of him only when they were immediately before the house. His mild and open look seemed to reassure them. They paused, taking his measure.

"Hello, friends," he said.

"Kalander!" cried Alyss. "What is this? What's all this talk we hear?"

"It will probably be as much of a surprise to me as it was to you. I've had a little shock already, a while ago. Why don't you come in? We'll have a little tea; kettle's on. Was hoping you might come up this way, actually."

They were relieved by his words and his manner; here was the old Kalander they had always known, steady and sensible. But they did not speak until he had set the tea before them at the table, and the silence was suspenseful and full of pain for them all.

"Now," he said. "Suppose you tell me what brings you here, and then I'll tell you what I know."

He wanted to keep Miranda's secret if he could.

"Well," said Strephon, "we were about to sit down to dinner, but we couldn't find Ginny and Miranda. We called, and first in flies Miranda, all alone, crying, and holding her hands over her face—"

"But smiling," said Alyss, as if puzzled.

"Yes, smiling, too," agreed Strephon. "And she wouldn't talk; she just ran to her room."

"And I went after her, to see what was the matter; but she wouldn't say. I asked her where Ginny was, and she said she didn't know, that she thought she had come back before her.

"Then Strephon calls me that Ginny's back. So I went down to put the dinner on the table."

"And here's little Ginny," said Strephon, "bursting with a secret. She said she saw you and Miranda kissing."

There was an abrupt silence at this. They had become upset again in the telling, and looked at him almost in accusation. Despite his compassion for their alarm, he thought of the little girl and her big secret and he suddenly laughed out loud.

They brightened up at the sound of his mirth.

"Oh, Kalander—it isn't true, is it?" begged Alyss.

"Finish your story," was all he would say.

They looked at each other.

"Well, we went and asked Miranda what the truth was," said Strephon. "And she said that she had kissed you. And she said she wasn't ashamed; and that she was in love with you, that she was going to marry you."

With this they succeeded in astonishing him. He sat staring at them for several minutes, speechless. No response could have reassured them more effectively.

Now Strephon laughed suddenly; and in a moment, Alyss, too, though she wept at the same time.

"I guess you were right when you said that you'd be as as surprised as we were," said Strephon.

Kalander gathered his wits.

"My friends," he said, "my old and dear friends—all I can say is that I had no idea this was happening. I have never thought of Miranda as other than a child, almost as my own child. She did kiss me—outside, about an hour ago—just once, and it's the only time she ever did. Till that moment I had no idea what was in her head. And till you said this about marrying me, I had no idea either." Tears started to his eyes as he thought of their pain, of the pain Miranda had yet to bear. "Believe me," he said, "if I had known she felt this way—if I had known . . ." He shook his head at the impossibility of his ever having conjectured what was taking place.

"None of us knew," said Strephon, already regretting that he was in part a cause of his friend's grief.

"No," agreed Alyss. "I certainly never dreamed it."

"Who would have?" wondered Kalander.

"But she says she's been in love with you for years," said Alyss, unable to keep the reproach out of her voice. "She said she's always intended to marry you."

This was almost funny; at least it made them all smile.

"Alyss," he said, "on my honor, I had nothing to do with this. I never encouraged her—never knowingly. I'm sure you know that. I'm only sorry she's gotten this fool idea into her head. What shall we do? I mean, here we are. I live here, you live there. We can't exactly stop being friends."

"I know," said Alyss. "I've already thought, maybe we could send her back to my sister's. But I'd be afraid she'd pine. I'd want to see how she was taking it."

"This is terrible," said Kalander, as the difficulty of the situation became clear to him.

They sat in mutual, worried silence for some minutes. Then Kalander spoke again.

"I tell you what," he said. "The most important thing we'll do is not tell anyone. We don't want the girl made a laughingstock for getting a crush on a man as old as her father. You send her up here to me, and I'll have a talk with her about this marrying business. I'll just tell her straight out that it's foolish and she's to put it out of her head. I'll tell her I love her, of course, but as a daughter, not a wife. Then we'll just have to let nature take its course. There'll be tears—it will hurt some, depending how infatuated she is; but she's young. By Christmas she'll be off with her friends again, having a good time."

They contemplated this plan and began to feel better. But then Alyss wept, instantly and violently.

"What's the matter?" asked Strephon, holding her.

Alyss did her best to explain between sobs. "She did so love reading that Greek," she said.

Miranda did not come until the next day. The three of them had settled on this; they knew it would require a good many explanations before she would be ready. At noon Kalander heard her step on the porch.

He composed himself. He guessed she would be embarrassed, red-eyed, perhaps sulky; he meant to overcome her hurt and defiance with gentle remonstrance.

But she was none of that. When he opened the door she smiled at him, as radiantly happy as ever.

*Dear God*, he exclaimed inwardly, *this is going to be a tougher business than I thought!*

She stepped over the threshold and closed the door behind her with a laugh. He had retreated, backing away in some confusion. "This time I'll watch out for prying little sisters," she said, smiling still. Then she stole close and kissed him.

"Miranda!" he said. "You mustn't do that!"

She laughed softly. "Why not?"

"Because it isn't right!"

Her hazel eyes were unconquerable; they shone with love that no repulse could discourage.

"Now, look, dear girl," he began, groping after the ideas and words he had thought over in the night and morning past. "This won't do. I'm old enough to be your father."

"That's an old story," she said, with a set to her lips both mocking and bewitching.

"Well, I practically am a kind of father to you. A godfather, I suppose."

"Don't be silly, Kalander. I've never looked upon you as a father. God made you to be my husband."

"Haven't your parents spoken to you? Haven't they told you how that can never be?"

She laughed again. At the sound something seemed to soften in him—his resolve, his will, his confidence in his understanding of the situation.

"Don't you see?" she said. "Think how wonderful it would be. You and I—we'd be perfect partners. You can't live alone, Kalander. You need help. Everyone does. I'm a good hand around the place—you ask Mama. Tell me you wouldn't like me to make your meals. Tell me you wouldn't like another pair of hands weeding with yours. And think of the evenings, the two of us, by the fire, reading through every book on the shelf. And when we finished them all, we'd start over again." She was weeping, slow, blissful tears.

He put his hand to his head, absolutely at a loss.

"Don't you think I'm even a little pretty, Kalander?" she asked.

Now he looked at her and he saw how beautiful she was. He had always seen it, in part; but it had always been a beauty that was hers alone, or was to be the joy of some husband someday; until she had put the idea into his head, he had never dreamed it could be his joy, and so had never fully perceived it.

"I think you're beautiful," he corrected her. His voice sounded awkward and hoarse to him.

"And I think you're the most handsome man that God ever made. *Kalander*, you know—you told me a long time ago what it means: a beautiful man. You *are* beautiful, Kalander. Your hands are beautiful, your face is beautiful—your shoulders, your arms, your back, Kalander—your voice, your voice is so beautiful . . ."

"Miranda," he said. He felt himself being drawn after her into something so utterly new and strange it frightened him. "I'm old, you're young. I know it sounds stupid, but it's true. I loved once; I've loved already. God gave me Greta; that was all I was given."

"But Greta's dead, and I'm alive; and I'm here, now, and I love you." She smiled still. "Don't you see?"

"Greta may be dead, but . . ."

"Don't you see?" she asked again, slipping forward once more and embracing him. Her arms held him tightly, her slim, strong form pressed against him, and she turned her face upward to his. "Which has more of a hold on you," she asked, "death or life?"

He made no answer.

She went softly away, a short distance from him. The radiance still glowed on her countenance.

"You may as well resign yourself," she laughed. "I won't let you go. I'll work on Mama and Papa, too."

At the mention of Strephon and Alyss he recalled what it was he was supposed to do.

"No," he said. "We won't marry, you and I. Your parents don't wish it. Think of their dreams for you, all these years—to marry a young man your age, to—"

"My parents can change their dream a little," she said.

"You stubborn thing! Won't you listen to me?"

"I'll only listen to one objection, Kalander."

"What's that?" he asked, eager and yet strangely fearful.

"Just tell me this—would you be sorry to marry a woman like me?"

He felt, dimly, that this was his only moment to do what had to be done.

"Yes," he said.

But his voice, his tone, was so patently a falsehood that she laughed when she heard it; and stood there before him, blushing and laughing, because she knew he was not telling the truth.

And he, now, was laughing too, at the foolishness of his fib.

"Go on," he said, surrendering to his mirth, "Get out of here. Get out, girl! You're impossible. Go tell your parents I can't do anything with you. It's up to them."

She seemed inclined to steal another kiss, but he motioned her away. At the door she paused.

"I'll see you tomorrow," she said.

She did come on the morrow, though not at the usual time. How she slipped away from her parents' house he did not know. She brought the book. At first he refused to let her in; but she promised that she would say nothing more of marriage or love—she wanted only to read, she said.

He thought about this for a minute or two behind the closed door. In the end he decided that it might be a good way to ease her out of a difficult situation. Perhaps if they were together again as they used to be, and there was no more talk of this infatuation, she would gradually give it up and forget it. Maybe in a few months she would laugh and blush at the recollection.

He found, however, when he let her in, that there were more ways to talk of love than words encompassed. They had only one book; it was an excuse for her to sit beside him; and her closeness, her serene assurance, her living, breathing beauty—all combined somehow to tell him that she loved him.

He could think on the Greek only with difficulty. Three days ago she had been a girl, sitting beside him; now she was a woman. He saw how the curls that escaped from her ribbons fell forward and touched her soft cheeks; he saw the long lashes flutter over the hazel eyes as she studied the page skillfully and cheerfully; he smelt the clean fragrance of her clothing and her skin. He was aware, now, of the blood within him—of his pulse, of the coming and going of the color in his weathered face.

*Kalander,* he thought, *what kind of a fool are you turning into?*

She kept her promise, and made no attempt to kiss him or hold him; but after she had left, he thought for a long time of the smile she had given him as she left, and how it had almost felt like a kiss.

The next day she was back again, again at an odd hour. He was busy turning up the garden. And though he resisted successfully her suggestion that they sit down together for a few minutes, he did not have the will to stop her from following him down the row with the book in her hands, reading to him. It did not matter that he feigned not to be paying attention; she was so good at the language now that she needed little correction.

This day was more painful to him than any other. The words of the poet were in his head—

> Thrice blessed are your father and lady mother,
> thrice blessed are your brothers—whose heart
> within them rejoices always, because of you,
> as they watch you, a fair young branch, joining the dance.
> But that man is blessed far beyond all
> who can give you every gift and take you as a bride
> to his own home.

And

> Nothing is better than this—
> when a like-minded man and woman
> keep house together.

Her voice rang about him like a haunting song; he could not but think how pleasant it would be to wake and hear her speak his name; how sweet to hear her say goodnight.

Finally he paused in his work. "Stop reading," he said abruptly.

She closed the book obediently and waited, smiling quietly.

"Get yourself a spading fork, if you want, and help me."

She flew to the shed and back, spat on her hands, and began to delve beside him.

It seemed the mould turned over at her behest. Strength coursed in him; down the rows they went, digging and turning side by side. Sweat dripped from his brow, and her fractious ringlets clung to her damp temples.

The sun was westering when they were done.

"Thank'ee," he said, looking over the work.

"You have no need to say thank'ee to me," she said, laughing. He looked at her glowing cheeks, her chest heaving with the exertion.

"You'd better go," he said.

She cleaned off the fork, returned it to the shed, took up the book again, and went past him on her way home. He refused to look at her until she stopped and said, "Kalander—might I borrow your handkerchief?"

He supposed she wanted to appear more present-able when she went into the house. He gave her his handkerchief, a square of coarse blue cloth. She wiped her brow and neck with it; then, while he watched, she slipped it into the bodice of her dress and ran away laughing, as if daring him to prevent her theft.

He grinned with a wild delight and turned away to hide his emotion.

Then he went back up to the house, to sit in stupe-faction over his bread and cheese.

Every day for a week she came. Sometimes they read; sometimes they worked together; sometimes they just sat. She said no other word aloud about her love, keeping the letter of her promise, at least; but it hardly mattered, since she broke the spirit of it. And he felt no more faithful, for he felt that he himself was not keeping his promise to Strephon and Alyss.

He became almost frightened of her. Or of what he felt when she came near. He shrank from her, and yet he would not go out of a certain orbit from her when she was with him. He had been so sure that all these feelings were dead in him that he could hardly recognize them when they began to call his name again.

He wanted badly to talk to Strephon and Alyss, but he did not dare go down to their house, for fear some scene would ensue there that he could not control.

One afternoon she came to him as usual. He said nothing to her, not one word; nor did he look at her. She read at first, but found he would not respond to the questions she put to him from time to time, so she stopped and sat in silence with him. This was worse than anything; for he heard her confident and trusting love speaking aloud in her silence and patience. He felt like Proteus in the grip of his foe; he could turn himself into any form, twist and writhe, and still she held, never doubting victory.

"I can't bear this," he said at last. He stood up and walked to the door. She followed him.

He went straight down the path out of the hollow. She matched his determined stride with her lighter tread. He did not look at her, or left or right; he went directly to the house of his friends.

He burst in. Or so he felt anyway. Alyss was beginning to make supper; Strephon was working on his traps. They looked at him strangely—almost, he thought, the way Miranda looked at him. The three little children perked up, realizing something interesting was taking place.

Strephon was the first to recover. He shooed Strephie and Turner and Genevra out to play in the woodshed. Then he gestured Kalander to a seat. Miranda took a stool next to their guest. Strephon sat, and Alyss came to the fireside too, wiping her hands on her apron.

Kalander did not know what to say; he did not know what to feel. He looked at his friends and thought how he loved them, and how he would not hurt them for anything; how he would gladly live alone for the rest of his life to avoid hurting them. But when he looked at Miranda, sitting beside him, he felt that he could not bear his situation any longer.

They were waiting for him to speak, and he could not. The three of them looked at him for some time, and grew a little puzzled that he did not say anything. Strephon seemed finally to understand why.

He laughed gently and looked at Alyss. She smiled. It was that same odd smile that Kalander did not understand.

"I think we've all got our friend in a hold," he said, "and he doesn't know which way to turn to get free."

"Well," said Alyss, "maybe we ought to let him go."

"I reckon," said Strephon.

He smiled at his hands, which he was rubbing lightly together in a bashful way.

"It's like this, Kalander," he said. "I guess we've come round. Miranda's held to it. I don't know how you feel; maybe we're not giving you the help you need. But if you and Miranda wanted to set up together, I guess we wouldn't mind it. We can't think of better man or a better woman. Seems like a sensible kind of thing. I mean, there is the difference in ages, but that will have to be borne—by her, and by you—later on. We all grow old. You might as well grow old with the one you love.—If you love her, I mean."

The three of them looked at him again, but again he could not speak, although now it was for a different reason. Miranda slipped off the stool and knelt beside him. She laid her hand on his sleeve, and he looked down on her eager face.

"I guess you win the match, girl," he said.

# The Healing

And you thought evil against me,
but God thought it for good.
>—Genesis 50:20

*Homo novit quod amor sit,*
*sed non novit quid amor est.*

People know *that* love is,
but not *what* love is.
>—Swedenborg

Par's wife ran away with a man from upcountry, leaving him with the farm and a son three years old. It was a matter everyone knew about; she was living with her lover at Crevisham, twenty miles the other side of the shire seat from Par's place. He waited many months, hoping that she would return; he loved her that much. Indeed, he went up to Crevisham several times to ask her to come home, but she would have none of him. Finally he went to the Elders, and made his case for a divorcement in proper form, hoping that would make her reconsider. Usually such matters take months, as the Elders satisfy themselves that in truth the marriage cannot be saved. To his surprise, they granted him the divorcing at once and without question. Indeed, everyone pitied him, because he was a gentle, loving man, well-liked in the shire, and clearly had been wronged.

Folks hoped he would give up on his wife and find another helpmeet soon, especially because of the child.

However, the divorcement was not complete, because by law the Elders had to let the marriage stand ten more days in case the wife gave up her lover.

On the tenth day but one it happened that she and the man set out in a light wagon to ride north, back to his shire. On the switchback over Saddle Notch the wagon overturned; the man jumped free, but Par's wife, Lilith, was caught under the wagon and broke her back. Word of this accident reached the Elders just before the session, and they stayed the divorcement until they could hear more.

When Lilith's lover discovered she would never walk again, he went away upcountry and left her in the place she had been taken to, a farmhouse near the Notch. A witness said that when the people at the farm reproached him for leaving, he declared angrily that he would have nothing more to do with a woman who would never walk again. The Elders accepted this as proof of his abandonment. There was then an idea that her kin could take her back, but they were proud people, and they disowned and repudiated her before the next session.

So the Elders sent word to Par that by law they could not give him the divorcement. A man could not divorce a woman who could not fend for herself, no matter what sins she had committed against him.

There was nothing for it but that Par take her home. And this, in fact, was what he wanted to do.

He went up and arranged for her care until the leech should say she could be moved. It was three months he paid these costs before she could be fetched back to his place in a wagon.

When they came up the road to the farm the neighbors went out to greet him. Lilith was groaning and crying out with each lurch of the leech's wagon. Par was riding alongside, straight in the saddle, his eyes fixed ahead, and the tears sliding down his cheeks unheeded. His neighbors stood mute by the road, realizing for the first time how deeply he still loved her.

After a time the pain abated. The leech said the bones had mended; but she still had no feeling below her waist.

Par did everything. He worked the land, he minded the child, he brought in the winter's wood, he cooked the meals and served them. His neighbors helped as they could, but it happened that that was a hard year for everyone. Sometimes a neighbor would come over early and take the child for the day. Par would sit down at the kitchen table, intending to take a minute to plan how to catch up on his tasks; like as not he would fall asleep there, sitting up, at eight o'clock in the morning.

Some whispered that it would be better if his wife took sick and died, as usually happened with paralytics. But he took too good care of her for that.

Once when he brought the little boy down to church someone said he looked near to breaking. He answered, his face expressionless: "No, I'm not near to breaking; not half near."

He had some strength that kept him going even though there seemed to be no hope; even though before him lay chores without end for his natural life, as bondservant to a woman who hated him. Folks said they did not know which would be the greater miracle, if she walked again or if she learned to love him.

In March of the next year Par heard of a new healer in the shire, a woman. The leech spoke against her, and all Par's neighbors took the part of the leech for some reason. But Par had nothing to lose. He sent for her.

She came up the lane to his place in a heavy cape made of black wool. Around her face was a muffler, for the chilly winds were still blowing. The little boy, Andros, saw her first and called his father to the window; together they watched the healer struggling against the March gusts.

"Tall," said Andy.

"That she is," said Par.

"Witch," said Andy.

"That she is not," said Par.

All the same, when she came in he realized why folk might be afraid of her. At first, when she had slammed the door closed and leaned against it, he was most conscious of her womanliness, her freshness, her vitality; but as she unwound the muffler he saw that her face bore disfiguring scars, as if from some horrible ritual.

"You are Par, are you not?" she asked him.

He could tell she was commonsensical from her tone. "Aye. Would you like to sit a minute?"

"No. I'll go to your wife straightaway."

He led the way up the stairs. Andy scrambled to stay with him, turning his wide eyes at every other step to peep at the big stranger.

Par knocked at the door and swung it open. Lilith was propped up in bed, staring at them, pale, with a spot of anger in each cheek. Par went in and stood at the foot of the bed; Andy hid behind him.

The healer came in more slowly, gazing evenly at Lilith.

Par watched them stare at each other for several minutes. He was surprised when the healer turned to him and looked into his eyes for as long a time. Just when he was about to break the silence, her eyes sought out little Andy. She put out a hand, a fist, turned knuckles up. Par noticed that her hand was very fine, white, and young; the blue veins ran through the skin on the back of it like faint threads of color beneath the surface of white stone.

Andy realized the gesture was an invitation. He stole forward and raised his open hands under the stranger's outstretched fist. The healer loosened her fingers, and a sweet fell into Andy's cupped palms. The boy glanced at his father, who nodded. He fell to sucking on the candy at once, sparing only one grateful glance to the witch.

"Well?" demanded Lilith.

"We must turn her over," said the healer to Par.

Together they laid Lilith flat on the bed and turned her on her belly. The healer drew up the long white nightgown she wore, drew it up to her shoulders, so that Lilith lay almost completely naked on the bed. She made a little angry noise.

Par looked at her and thought how beautiful she was still, even after the accident, even after lying here for all this time without moving, even after another man had used her and cast her aside. Suddenly he saw that the healer was watching him, and he colored, feeling ashamed of his thoughts.

Then, however, the healer began rubbing, prying, thumping along Lilith's spine, buttocks, and legs. Her movements were brisk, methodical, businesslike. Finally she tickled Lilith with a feather she had produced from a pocket of her long skirt—first on the soles of her feet, then behind her knees, then on her privates. It was almost as if she suspected Lilith might be shamming; but she seemed to prove to her own satisfaction that such was not the case.

She pulled down the nightgown again. At her sign, Par helped her turn Lilith over and prop her on the pillows.

"Well?" demanded Lilith angrily once more.

The healer eyed her expressionlessly, then turned deliberately to Par, ignoring his wife.

"It will take warm water," she said, speaking in a low, firm voice. "She must be immersed in it and moved about. Twice a day, for about a half hour. Every day for—as long as it takes."

"But will I walk again?" asked Lilith.

"I don't know. Maybe, maybe not."

"If you don't know—"

"My God, where will I get this warm water?" exclaimed Par suddenly. "Where will I put so much of it?"

"Do you have a cistern?"

"No."

"Then you must make one. A big one."

"Get out!" said Lilith. "I won't listen to you! The leech says you know nothing, and I believe him!"

The healer ignored her pointedly, as if she were no more capable of discussion than a sick cow lowing fretfully in a stall.

"I'll show you where to dig the cistern," said the healer to Par. "When I come back."

"How will I do that?" he said, thinking of the digging, and overwhelmed. "The ground is still frozen. And when it thaws, I must plow and plant—"

"You'll do it," said the healer.

He knew she was right. He would do it.

He followed her down to the door.

"What do I owe you?" he said, as she prepared to go out into the wind again. "Don't you want to stay and warm yourself?"

"No," she said. "As for payment . . ." She paused and peered through the little look-see in the door. "What is that shed at the end of the lower field?"

"My father once kept harness in it. I don't use it now."

"When the weather warms, I'll be back. I'll live in that shed. I'll take one-fourth of what your garden bears, a fourth of the fields, a fourth of the orchards. A fourth of the chickens, the eggs, the milk, and any pigs or cattle that you slaughter. I'll stay here and help you heal her."

He was aghast. "A fourth!" he said. Then: "But you *will* heal her?"

"*You* must heal her," she corrected him firmly. "She cannot do it. I cannot do it. Only you can do it."

She opened the door.

"And you, too," she said, "you have to have your healing." He furrowed his brow, not comprehending; but she did not explain.

"I'll be back in the spring," she said, and went away.

The healer came to stay on the very day he picked the first peas from the garden. He weighed out a fourth of the pods and gave them to her. He lent her a broom and all else she needed, and she cleaned out the shed and set up housekeeping in it.

Thereafter she was on the farm almost all the time. She weeded the garden, minded Andy, chased the crows, and oversaw the building of the cistern. The only things she would not do were care for Lilith or work in the house. Although it hurt when he had to give up a quarter of his produce to her—for it was his cash-quarter, and it would leave him with nothing to sell—he began to think he had not done badly by the deal. Even with the extra work of digging the cistern pit and lining it with mortared stones, the farm began to flourish. He almost wondered about witchcraft: he had never seen the corn grow so high, so green, so eager. The quickgrass faded out of his garden, the slugs were nowhere to be seen, and even his old enemy the woodchuck shifted camp to a neighbor's land after the healer cast a ball of something down its earth.

Her name was Philomela. She strode around the farm, doing the chores, an image of steadiness and strength. He would look up from mixing a pail of mortar as she went by, Andy tagging along behind her, and almost smile with a kind of puzzled gratitude. As for her, she seldom, if ever, betrayed any emotion; she was all business. Except, he noticed, that she was very kind and sweet to Andy when she thought Par out of sight or hearing. A pity, he thought, that her face was so scarred.

When folks heard what she was doing for Par, they began to think maybe the leech was wrong. One by one they began to come to her when the leech was not handy; and when her cures worked, she built her following. Some said it was the best thing that could have happened to Par—it was almost like having a real wife instead of that vicious thing that lay useless in the bedroom upstairs, poisoning the household. They might have whispered about imagined goings-on between Par and Philomela; but when they saw the healer's face, they knew no man would take up with her.

It came that Par began to dread market days; for then Philomela would be absent, borrowing his wagon and taking her quarter to town. It was not just that he had to carry all the work on his own back as before. He missed her quiet presence and assurance about the place. She seemed to do well in selling his meat and vegetables; she brought back not so much as a single bean unsold. Par could often hear the jingle of the coins in her pocket as she unharnessed the horse.

He finished the cistern about mid-June. When he was just pointing up the stonework tightly to hold the water, Philomela came to the edge and examined it.

It was about twelve feet long and six feet wide, about six deep. At one end were broad stone steps. At the other was an overflow and a runoff to take the water away down hill. Philomela had dowsed and found a spring he had never known existed; he had then built the cistern below it, and thus would be able to pipe off the spring water and fill the cistern without carrying a single bucket. It was a curious fact that the water on his land seemed unusually high this year, though his neighbors were complaining that their wells were already low.

"What do you think?" he asked.

"You've done beautiful work," she said. He was surprised at her praise.

She sat down on the rim of the cistern. Andy had fallen asleep in the orchard—he often took a nap in the afternoons—so they were alone.

"If it's worth doing," he began, but he faltered as he saw her expression.

"It's worth doing well," she finished for him. He thought maybe she was mocking him, but he was not sure. "Is that why you've taken such pains with this work?"

"I suppose," he said, though suddenly he was not sure.

"No, Par," she said. "It's because you love your wife."

He considered this, hanging his head haggardly.

"Suppose I do," he said. "What of it? Shouldn't a man love his wife?"

"Not a man who has been treated as you have. Have you ever really thought about why you love a woman who despises you?"

He darted a despairing look at her, but did not answer.

"Has she ever loved you?"

"I once thought so. Now I don't know. I think she always hated me."

"I want an answer, Par. Why do you love her?"

He swallowed hard; he would not look at the healer. "She's so beautiful," he said finally.

"That she is," said Philomela. "In all my days, in all my travels, I have never seen a woman more beautiful than she is."

"You think so?" said Par, looking up almost eagerly.

"Her face is like something carved—too beautiful to be real. And her body . . . I've not a man's eye for it, but I can guess what it would make a man feel, looking at it."

"Aye," he murmured, leaning back against the stones where the mortar was dry.

She, too, leaned back, propped on her hands.

"Let me tell you a story, Par."

"All right."

"I knew of a man once who bought land with his wife's dower. It was a beautiful place. A fine house, broad fields, and good hardwood—plenty of walnut and cherry; this was down southern way. He had to borrow money in addition to the dower. He lived there for five years. He loved that land. He was like a fellow in a fairy tale who wakes up in a magic castle, with everything he ever desired. Well, one day the castle blew away in a puff of smoke. Some trouble fell between him and his wife; she got a divorcement, and demanded her dower back. Then his creditors came for their money too; and the upshot was he had to sell out. When I was called to him, he was broken and sick. It was not losing his wife so much, it was losing the land that was killing him. He kept saying that to me: 'My land, my land—I had the finest land on God's earth, and I lost it.' And I said to him, 'You didn't have the land. You were just borrowing it from your wife and your creditors.' After he looked at it that way, he started to get better. It was the idea that he'd lost something beautiful that was killing him. When he realized he had never really had it, his hurt could heal.

"You're like that man, Par. When you married Lilith, you thought you owned the most beautiful thing on earth. But you didn't own it. She just gave you the borrowing of it for a little while, and even that probably not with much good will. Then she took it back and gave it to someone else."

"But he didn't want her," said Par angrily.

"That's why she loved him," said Philomela. "She loved him because he was the kind of man who scorns everyone. So long as she was with him, she felt she was winning out against his scorn. With her beauty she was making him need her. And that made her feel her power. She likes to feel her power. That's why she never cared about you; because you never scorned her."

He stared at her. He could not follow the twisting paths of her thoughts, but all the same he learned them, and he knew he would find himself following them again in his own mind, in the days to come.

"You," continued Philomela, "you tried to do the same thing with her. You always wanted to make her love you. You wanted to conquer her scorn for you."

"That's not true," he protested, almost desperately.

"No? Let me ask you, Par: Why are you taking such good care of her? Why have you built this splendid cistern?"

"Because it's the law," he said. "Because it's the decent thing to do. Because you told me to do it. Because if she could walk again, life wouldn't be so hard for me. She could do some of the chores—at least she could mind the child."

"If she can walk, she can run. And if she can run, she can run away."

"No," he said. "She'll not run away again. She's learned her lesson."

"Neither of you has learned your lesson," said Philomela. Then, while he watched her moodily, she stood up and went away to the orchard.

When the cistern was full, Par found, the water warmed quickly in the morning sun. One mid-morning in late June, Philomela said the water was warm enough, and bid Par bring Lilith down.

He went up by himself to her bedroom. The instant he entered, Lilith knew why he was there.

"I won't go," she said.

"It's for your good. Don't fight it, Lilith. It's the only hope we've got."

"I won't do it. It's a plan you hatched up with that witch to drown me and have done with me."

"Come on, Lil, I've just about killed myself making that cistern. Try it just once—"

"Go to hell!" she said. She threw her arms behind her and gripped the posts of the bed with both hands. He tried to pick her up, but she lashed out at him and struck him.

He went outside again. Philomela was waiting by the cistern. He saw she had a length of strong cord in her hand.

"She won't come," he said. "She struck me when I tried to pick her up."

Without a word Philomela handed him the cord.

He went back and threatened Lilith with being tied. The threat meant nothing to her; he had to tie her wrists together and lash them to her waist. He was a very strong man; she seemed surprised at his strength. Then he carried her down the stairs and outside, while she resisted as best she could, weeping angrily and cursing him with the foulest words she knew.

When he brought her to the cistern, Philomela, too, seemed to grow angry. "She must be naked," she said sternly. "Strip her, Par."

"You slut!" shouted Lilith, spitting at Philomela. "I won't go in the water! I won't be stripped!"

"Have you no shame, woman? Your child sees your madness," said Philomela. She pointed to where a little face was peering fearfully out of a window in the house.

"What difference does it make whether she wears a gown or not?" asked Par. "She'll get just as wet."

"All the difference in the world," Philomela said. "Strip her."

He obeyed, though it meant untying the cord and starting over again. Lilith resisted him even more fiercely, clinging to the gown so that he nearly had to tear it from her grasp. After he jerked the gown off over her head, she began to sob bitterly, humiliated and frustrated at her helplessness.

"I'm sorry," he said to her. The tears stood in his eyes as he looked upon her beautiful, broken body.

"Don't pity her, Par," said Philomela. "She brought this on herself."

"Do I have to tie her again?" he asked.

"No, no!" cried Lilith. She was afraid of going into the water bound.

He picked her up and carried her down the steps into the cistern. As the water rose about them both she gripped him tightly, screaming with terror; in his pity for her the tears streamed down his face.

He was not sure what he should do. Suddenly Philomela was beside him, standing tall in the clear water, fully clothed but for her shoes, which she had kicked off at the top of the steps.

Between the two of them they managed to persuade Lilith to relax. Philomela showed him how to move Lilith's legs about and draw her about the cistern. The water seemed to have a calming effect on her; or perhaps her emotion had exhausted her.

"That should do for this morning," said Philomela after some time. Par took Lilith into his arms again and carried her out of the cistern and into the house. He laid her on the bed still wet—he was dripping himself—and rubbed her dry with a clean cloth.

She lay on her back, immobile, staring at nothing, on the verge of sleep already. Suddenly he felt desire for her; he could hardly look at her, she was so beautiful. He drew up the covers and went heavily out of the room.

Philomela was still standing by the cistern. Her wet clothes clung to her figure; she was now chilly and her nipples showed through the cloth of her dress. Par turned from the sight with a groan.

"What's the matter, Par?" asked Philomela.

"It makes all of this even worse for me if she's naked," he said.

"Good," she said.


They went through the ritual again that afternoon and twice every day, rain or shine. One day that summer Par twisted his ankle in an old stump hole and Lillith thought that she would have a reprieve; but Philomela picked her up, as easily as if she were the child, and carried her into the cistern herself.

Lilith gave up resistance. She came to enjoy the attention it cost the others to care for her. If Par was late she shouted from her room, nagging him. In the water, she lay back with her eyes closed, luxuriating in the role of spoiled and pampered royalty. She noticed, too, that Par was troubled by his desire for her, and she teased him cruelly. She vented her continual pique at Philomela by taunting her for her scars, calling her an ugly crow and a witch. Par could bear her tormenting him, but when she spoke ill to Philomela, he rebuked her sharply. This, of course, only made her laugh.

All this time Par had been sharing the one bed with Lilith. It was the only bed in the whole house. Now he found that his desire for her troubled him so much he could not sleep, even though he was exhausted at the end of the day. He began sleeping in the kitchen; and here one dawn Philomela found him when she came to borrow the broom.

"I couldn't sleep," he explained, sitting up and rubbing his face.

"Don't worry," she answered. "The fever's always worst before it breaks."

Par and Philomela were in the corn, harvesting. Andy lay snoozing in the shade of the wagon. Market day was tomorrow, and Philomela wanted to take her quarter of the corn this week.

A faint cry came to them—"Par! Par!"—repeated on the leaden air of late summer. Par and Philomela looked at one another. The sound was strange; it was not like Lilith's usual nagging. It seemed joyful. "Par! Par! Come quickly!"

With one final look at Philomela, Par put away his knife and trudged back to the house. The call came again; he was sure now that it was a happy one; he was curious and puzzled, but he had not the energy to speed his step.

Up in the bedroom, Lilith motioned him to her. She was smiling radiantly; when he was within reach she pulled him down and clung to his neck. He sensed that she was wildly excited, her pulse racing, her breathing rapid.

"I can feel the sheet on my toes," she whispered.

He burst into tears, embraced her, and kissed her repeatedly. She laughed and kissed him back.

"Show me," he said. She nodded, grinning.

He pulled back the covers. "Close your eyes," he commanded. "Now, tell me when I've touched your foot." He paused a moment, then tickled the end of her big toe.

"Now," she said. Her eyes opened and she smiled brightly.

"I'm going to tell Philomela," he said.

"Oh, Par," she said.

"What?"

"I'm going to walk again!"

"It won't be long, I know it."

She motioned him close again, and he approached her. "What?" he asked.

She pulled him down and kissed him again, a deep kiss, full of desire, full of life. "It won't be long," she whispered.

He went away dizzily. When he came to where Philomela was, he was grinning.

"Well?" she said, keeping on with her work even as she spoke.

"She has feeling in her feet again," Par said.

"Is that all?"

"No, that's not all. By God, Philomela, I think she's going to love me at last."

She bowed her head over the cutting, but he could read the sharp pity in her face.

Within five weeks of that day, Lilith was walking about again. Philomela stayed on the farm until the last of the harvest was in and she had made her final trip to market. Then she told Par she was moving on. She would not tell him where. She said she would see him again. In her words to him she was impassive; but when Andy mourned and cried, Philomela wept too, although she smiled through her tears, and soothed the child, and promised him they would be together again soon. "Now, Andros," she said finally, "I want you to stay here in the house with your mother. Your father's going to walk me to the gate. You be ready to wave to me from the window when I wave to you." Andy went inside as he was bid. Philomela turned toward the gate, and Par went with her.

"Par," she began, "tell me what you're feeling."

He struggled to know even one part of what he felt, and could say nothing.

"All right, then, tell me this: Do you and your wife—" She hesitated. He had never seen her at a loss for words.

"Yes," he confessed, thinking to save her from her difficulty.

"And how do you feel about that?"

"It's strange. I've wanted it so badly, and I enjoy it. But I still feel . . ."

"Yes?"

"That I don't have all of her love yet."

He tried to read her face; she might have been glad, as she was glad when her cures were working, or she might have been grieved on his behalf, he could not tell. She might have been both.

They came to the gate in silence and faced each other.

"One more question, Par. A personal one. One about me."

"Yes?"

She seemed shy. She looked down, away. He had never seen this aspect of her. Finally she asked her question, almost blurting it out: "Do you think a man would ever kiss someone like me?"

He was amazed. But instantly, naturally, without thinking for a moment of her disfigurement, he caught her close to him and kissed her warmly on the lips.

She blushed. "I was only asking," she said. "I didn't mean for you to do it." Was that a tremble in her voice?

He laughed. "Then I've finally taught *you* something," he said. "Don't go around asking men questions like that."

"Normally I don't stand in any danger of answers like yours," she said. She waved to Andy.

"Goodbye," she said to Par.


Two weeks later, while Par was away for a day helping a neighbor, Lilith went before the session of the Elders and sued for a divorcement.

It was a curious case. The old divorcement had been, as it were, suspended, and the Elders were ready to grant it now on the old grounds, except that the old grounds no longer applied. Par was in such shock when he learned what she had done that he vowed he would not contest the action. He felt as if the roof beam had just fallen in on him.

So the Elders granted the divorcement almost at once. Two months after Philomela had left, Par and Lilith were no more husband and wife. Then Lilith sued to have the land sold, since Par could not pay her for it. He had made her joint tenant when they were married, although the land had always been in his family;

he had at that time been worried that if he died, a brother or sister of his would lay claim to it and take it from his wife. By March she had found a buyer for the place. The fellow made a point of telling Par that he especially liked the new cistern.

Thus by the end of the next winter Par found he had lost wife, home, and family. His share of the sale went to cover debts he had incurred in his own name while struggling to maintain the place during Lilith's illness. He could not help but think of the story Philomela had told him, of the man who had lost his land; it now made a double echo in his life.

He did have one consolation. Although at first Lilith had taken Andros with her, for the sake of appearances, she soon grew tired of caring for him, and left him for Par to see to. She herself went upcountry after her old lover. The last Par heard, the man had taken her back and they were spending her money at a merry rate.

Fortunately it was spring when Par had to give up the farm. He put his plow, his tools, and what remained of his household goods in the wagon, hitched up the horse, tied the cow along behind, and set Andy on the seat, to ride while he walked. He had no idea where to go. Andy thought it all a lark, and Par was intent on concealing his fears from the boy, so he played along.

He went south about ten miles, where the country opens up on the sea. He had heard land was cheap there, because the climate was cooler in the summer, and crops slower to grow. Not that he could have bought land at any price; but he hoped something would open up for him.

In talking to some travelers he met on the road, he found out that there was a healer living on a hill by the sea. He wondered if it might be Philomela; the wonder grew into a need to know; and soon he had found his way to the place.

It was wild land. Vast firs and crowded birches covered the broad hillslope. Leaving his wagon behind, he took Andy by the hand and went along the rough woods road that led uphill. On all sides was a dank darkness amid fir trunks so thick one could hardly have walked among them. "How'd you like to pull all those stumps, eh, Andy?" he said.

"Hard work, Dad," the boy agreed.

The trail went through a small clearing. As they entered it, they saw that a little shelter had been built here; and just coming out of the entrance was Philomela. Andy shrieked with glee and tore himself away from Par; woman and child met, laughing and crying; and then the healer came to Par.

She was smiling. She seemed almost radiant. He wondered why he had ever thought her scars disfiguring; now he did not notice them. Instead he saw her strength, her wisdom, her vitality.

"How are you?" she asked.

The pain was present again, instantly, at her question; he wept. "She went back to him," he said. "She went back to the same one who left her."

"Of course she did. So did you. Didn't she break your back and leave you for dead the first time? And you let her do it all over again."

He thought for a minute, downcast; but he made no response.

"Let's go up the trail," she said to him. "It's worth the climb."

They came out in a ragged meadow. When Par turned and looked back, he could see the ocean spread out below him, blue, winking with infinite flecks of light. He felt he had been here before, and yet he never had.

Andy scampered about, chasing the butterflies that drifted in the sea breeze and plucking spring flowers.

"What do you say?" asked Philomela. "Have you been healed, Par?"

"I can feel my toes again, at least," he said.

She laughed at his grimness.

"I bought this land with my fourth of your work. How do you like it?"

"Very much. You did well. You've a lot of hard work ahead of you, though, clearing and building."

She smiled at him until he could not help smiling back at her.

"Would you like to go halves with me?" she asked.

# Beneath the Wheel



A saint is only a sinner who has not been tempted.

—Proverb

The soul attracts that which it secretly harbors;
that which it loves, and also that which it fears; it
reaches the height of its cherished aspirations; it
falls to the level of its unchastened desires,—and
circumstances are the means by which the soul
receives its own.

—James Allen

## I

Colen was the miller on the near side of the mountain. He was a handsome man, lean, large-boned, and strong, with a shock of golden hair often streaked with the white dust of his trade. Despite the claim he might have made to good looks, he had little vanity for his appearance.

In his righteousness, however, he took some pride. He knew right from wrong as well as he knew in which direction the sun rose and in which direction it set. It was true that like sunup and sundown, his sense of right had shifted slightly with the seasons of his life, but it had remained in general the same. He was always outspoken in condemning any serious deviation from the law of God, of the land, or of human decency. In testimony to his righteousness, some of his neighbors brought their disputes to him, instead of going before the law. He took their trust both as a charge and a compliment, and judged their differences with intelligence and justice.

Yet this Colen went wrong. When he looked back, it seemed to him that he did not do so at any particular moment, although it was true that there was a point at which it became too late for him to stop himself. It was like those times when, after a long stint in the mill, he realized that the vague ache he had been feeling on his shoulder all day was an injury the great gearwheel had dealt him, leaving a livid bruise, though he might have little or no recollection of the instant he received the initial hurt. In the same way, he was not sure when his trouble began, but in the end the dark spot in his life was there for all to see.

Perhaps it started on the day when he first felt that odd rankling toward his wife. He was sweeping the old rotten flour out of the cracks in the granite steps of the mill, and he looked over to where Phyllis kept her skeps of bees; he saw her moving about there, in her quiet, capable way; and he felt a deep and unreasoning irritation with her.

He felt it again later, when he came into the house at the end of the day. She put his meal before him and sat with him while he ate, mothering their three children even while she listened to his commentary on the customers and how the weather would affect trade. Her voice was soft, and she smiled to lighten his mood; but he felt a strong revulsion for her.

Perhaps it was from that night on that he ceased to feel any desire for her. It was true that he still made love to her from time to time, but only as if from a need that had nothing to do with her person; and her kisses and little compliances he could not bring himself to answer. She felt the change in him; but he dodged her gentle questioning so well that for a long while she thought it was just a mood, a mood that would change with the wind.

He brooded on his discontent for some time before it struck him how odd it was, and how unjust. Phyllis had done him no wrong. It was almost as if she had done him too much right—as if she were too correct, too capable, too sincere in every duty. Her love for him was flawless, and even taking into account the frictions of everyday life, she was consistently thoughtful and cheerful towards him. And yet this irked him. Within the unbroken circle of her love he felt bound and captive.

Worse still, he felt bored.

2

These feelings grew on him through a spring and summer. He saw how Phyllis had noticed them; he found her watching him from time to time surreptitiously; he could feel her eyes on him when he sat by the window or the fire, his body still but his mind restless. She did not confront him. He almost wished she would. He wanted to accuse her—of what, he was not sure. Perhaps of being even more righteous than he was. Or perhaps he was angry at her because he knew his distaste for her was unjust.

He was in this frame of mind when one day a stranger from the far side of the mountain came to the mill. His name was Portius. He was young, but his face was hardened and lined by toil. He seemed to have an idea that if he took the extra trouble and expense to have his grain ground first, he could find a ready market for it with the rafters who took freight down the river. Colen, dubious of this, tried to dissuade him; but Portius was insistent. He had, he said, family at home that deserved better than he could offer them at present. He would accept the risk in the hope of a bigger return.

Colen pitied something in him. Fortune seemed to have him under the edge of her chisel, making a hone of him. Though Colen had more than enough to do in this season without his taking on work from another district, he took the grain and said he would do the work when he could.

After the job was finished, however, word came to him that Portius had broken his leg. Colen's pity stirred him again; and one day he loaded Portius's flour on his own wagon and set out to return it himself.

He asked the way as he went. To his surprise, Portius's house proved to be not far distant. The folks on the other side of the mountain formed another community altogether, and seemed rather than truly were remote.

The man owned a small steading that lay along the river. Rocks like whales rising to breathe surfaced in fields ragged with weeds—the land was clearly too much for one farmer to keep up. The garden was hopeless in comparison to Phyllis's. Although the house showed in a dozen pending repairs an evidence of the owner's will to improve it, here too hopes and intentions obviously outstripped resources and skills.

The door was ajar. Colen knocked on the doorpost, and a thin voice called to him from some inner room. He found his way through a small kitchen. On the table were signs of bread baking and other household chores interrupted. Beyond was a bedroom; in it, Portius was stretched out on a bed, the sweat dripping from his brow, his fingers clutching the bedclothes like claws as the pain wracked him.

"You!" he said wonderingly, as if he was not sure if what he saw was a trick of the fever or not.

"I got your message," said Colen. "I thought I might help you if I brought your flour."

"You brought my flour?"

"It's out in my wagon."

"Thank God! The raftmen want it by day after tomorrow."

"Can they get the sacks from your barn all right?"

"No—they have to be in the shed down by the water. Go find my wife. She'll show you where to put them." He turned his head weakly to the window beside the bed and called, "Cyn! Cyn!"

"Don't trouble yourself," said Colen. "I'll find her."

"She went to the well. It's such a hot day."

Colen nodded politely. The weather was actually rather cool.

He went outside and surveyed the place. A path skirting one of the fields showed him where the well must be; this he followed, and in a moment came upon a woman and a toddling child.

Her beauty was striking. Her hair was irridescently black; she defied the custom of all practical housewives by wearing it loose upon her shoulders as if she had just taken it down for sleep. When she raised her startled face to his, he saw that her dark eyes were set with brows and lashes like the perfect features of a painted doll; her lips were curved in the lines of the proverbial bow resting upon its taut string. The lacings of her bodice were loose, as if she had not had time since she had drawn her dress on that morning to perform even this small attention to herself; and yet in this she did not seem slovenly, but rather an object of sympathy. In small, strained hands she held the handles of two heavy buckets filled with water. She seemed altogether underbuilt for such work.

"You must be Cyn," he said.

"Cynthia," she answered. The little one began to wail, terrified of the stranger.

"My name is Colen. I'm the miller down round the mountain. I've brought your flour. Your husband said you might show me where to put it."

She struggled to comprehend; surprise and relief came over her features together.

"You brought the flour? My God, you've saved us! We had no idea how we were going to get it here in time."

He stepped forward without another word and took the buckets from her. She gathered up the child, smiling, and gazing at him with a gratitude that could not seem to get its fill.

"Show me the way," he said.

As he was finishing the task of unloading the flour Cynthia came down to the shed. He ignored her until he had set the last sack in its place. Then she stepped forward; he saw she was carrying a pitcher and a large mug. The scent of cider was all about her.

"My husband told me to bring you this."

"Very kind of you," he said. He took the mug and drank. It was not as good as Phyllis's cider, but the company of this beautiful woman made the flavor more pleasing; she watched him drink with her dark eyes, eyes that seemed now to know some secret.

"You're from Stooks, aren't you?" she asked.

He was surprised. "Yes. But I left there when I was five."

"You look so like one of my old neighbors. Alphen was his name."

"Alphen is my cousin! He was a neighbor of yours?"

"Your cousin!"

"You must be one of the Carter girls."

"I am."

There followed mutual expressions of amazement, even though Stooks was but a small place.

"Don't you miss it?" asked Cynthia.

"What, Stooks?—No, I can't say I do."

"But people are so different here. Don't you think? Less . . . friendly."

It seemed to him suddenly that he knew what she meant. He thought of Phyllis for some reason. "Oh," he said, "I guess that's true."

"Now if you hadn't been from Stooks, you never would have brought us our flour."

"Oh, I don't know," he said.

"My husband's from here. He says I'm too friendly. He says people don't understand that kind of thing around here. I think he's just jealous. He wants me to spend every second of every day thinking about him. He's even jealous of the baby."

"I know the kind of man you mean. But I can see why he might be worried that other men would be drawn to you." He felt it was obvious how he was laboring to work in the compliment, but he went on anyway. "You certainly are very beautiful."

"Oh," she demurred, shaking her head; but her lips, curving upward at the ends, formed the hint of a pleased smile that belied her modesty. She half-leaned and half-sat against some of the bags of flour near him—she was close, too close to him; he thought for an instant how he might put his arm around her shoulders; it was as if she had placed herself within the circle of his protection.

"More cider?" she asked.

He felt little need for it, but to prolong this strangely warm moment he held out the mug again. As she filled it she said, "It's good, isn't it? Isn't it the best cider you ever had?"

"It's among the best," he lied. And even as he did so, he wondered at himself. She detected his hesitation.

"Isn't it all right?"

"It's fine."

She caught at his hand, the hand that held the mug, with her own small hand, and brought the cider to her lips. Having tasted it, she smiled, reassured.

He raised the mug to his mouth again. It seemed suddenly different—crisp, cold, bubbling. It moved into his blood the way a roving bully moved through a schoolyard. As he drank it he thought of her mouth, of her mouth touching the rim of the mug, of the touch of her hand on his.

There seemed to be an aura around them, a stillness.

They talked. It did not seem to matter what they said. Their talk was gentle; it was warm and courteous, lit especially in those times and topics when she smiled. She said his wife must be happy in her life with him; and he found a way, with a twist of his mouth, to tell her that he was not happy in his life with her. He spoke of how he had felt a strong compassion for Portius the first time he had seen him; and he learned that the man was not above striking this delicate woman in his jealous rages. They spoke of Alphen, of Stooks, of how they had come to these parts. They spoke of the business of life, of putting food on the table for their families.

But at length they grew aware that they should go back to their duties. He shifted; she rose and took the empty mug. They smiled at one another. As she went before him to the door, she walked with a lingering step that kept her close to him, within his physical reach, as if at any moment she might stop and he might find himself holding her in one arm against his chest.

He climbed onto the seat of the wagon. He cast about for something to say, but he could not find any simple fashion to express his pleasure in her presence, his wish to see her again.

She, however, found a way to say these things to him: she reached up and caught his hand, and held it for a moment in her own, smiling softly at him.

For the first part of the way home he said to himself that he would tell Phyllis what a fine woman this Cynthia was. His wife would take an interest in her, perhaps befriend her, and help her in her difficult situation.

But then the possibility that Phyllis would do this irked him. He felt that she would spoil the bond he had with Cynthia—that with Phyllis near, he and Cynthia would not be able to talk, to look at one another as they had today.

It was only as he arrived home and saw Phyllis wave and blow him a kiss from the orchard, where she was cleaning an empty hive while the children played about her, that he felt a pang of guilt. Had he done wrong?

No. What wrong was there in talking? He had said and done nothing improper.

The more he thought about it, the more he was sure he never would do anything improper. His interest in Cynthia was not like that. They had certain sympathies, certain difficulties in common. There was nothing wrong in that.

When Colen lay in bed that night he kept his left hand on his forehead for a long while. It was the hand that Cynthia had held.

Beside him Phyllis slept, unconscious of what he felt. She had fallen asleep resting her hand lightly on his upper arm, but he had felt peevish beneath her touch—it was trusting, and its implicit affection was a reproach to his thoughts, which did not want to stay at home, but wished to roam back to the steading beyond the mountain. He pushed her hand away after he was sure she was asleep; she withdrew it with the same motion he had seen her use once when one of her bees had stung her on the palm, a gesture of puzzlement at betrayal, curling it in a loose fist and holding it against her breasts.

He thought of that black hair, of the lips like a bow, of the unlaced bodice; and Phyllis, with her pale gold hair, her thin lips, her clean nightdress buttoned about her neck, Phyllis seemed so pallid by comparison.

Rolling on his side, he put his back to his wife.

3

Four days later Colen came out of the house after supper and headed for the mill to close it up for the night. The sun was setting, but already the east was lit with the radiance of the moon, just above the horizon; it was almost full. He went slowly, brooding on vague unhappinesses.

A shadow stirred on the steps of the mill as he approached. He saw with astonishment that it was Cynthia; she was crouching against the door, waiting for him.

She rose when she saw him. She tried to draw herself up, to toss her head with some dignity; but her bravado faltered, and she looked only frail and hurt. He saw she had been crying, and her whole bearing told of pain.

"What is it?" he asked, amazed.

"May I talk to you?"

"Of course—of course you may."

He stood for a moment more in his uncertainty, and then stepped past her and thrust open the door of the mill.

It was very dark within, but some moonlight found its way through a dusty window. Cynthia groped her way forward and came up against some of the ubiquitous sacks; sank down upon them, and looked at him (he could barely see her) with appeal in her shadowed eyes. He closed the door and found his way near her.

The smell of apples rose from her. She crept close to him, closer.

"That thing," she said fearfully, looking up at the gearwheel overhead, whirling and creaking. "Does it ever stop?"

"Only in the dead of winter, when the river's frozen."

"How can you stand it?"

"You get used to it. After a while, you don't even hear it."

She tugged at her dress and pulled her sleeve down off her shoulder. Even in the faint light he could see the welt there on her pale flesh.

She looked up at him, appealing to him whether this was not wrong, what had been done to her; and crept within his arm, which he put gently around her; and she laid her head on his chest.

"I had to talk to you," she said. "I knew you would understand. I knew because you're from Stooks."

"Yes," he murmured vaguely. He hardly knew what was happening. She must have been making applesauce from the last windfalls—her scent was all tang and sweetness, mixed with the womanly smell of her, the crying smell.

She talked to him. She told him how Portius had raged at her for no reason and thrown his crutch at her. She had left the little one with a neighbor, but she had to talk to him, to Colen; no one else would understand.

He said things, but they meant nothing. They were just sympathetic sounds, yet they were all she needed. She talked the hurt out of herself in a confused monologue.

Somewhere in it all he kissed her hair. She raised her face to his, offered her face to his, and he kissed her. She seemed to take strength from his affection; she put her arms about him and pressed closer.

"I'm selfish," she said suddenly.

"No," he answered.

"I'm doing all the talking. You could probably say a few things too, about your wife. I know she's not good to you."

"Oh, she's good to me," said Colen bitterly. "She's too good to me."

"Too good?"

He tried to tell her, to express the revulsion he felt for Phyllis. He talked for some time, saying foolish things that did not add up.

She silenced him with a kiss. "Hush," she said. "I understand."

For a long while after that they did not speak; they remained, holding one another, as if afraid to move for fear of losing the peace they had found.

Finally she stirred and stood. "I'd better go," she said.

"Yes," he agreed. He went with her to the door; but before he could open it she stopped him, and took his hands in hers, and raised them to her lips, and kissed them; and kissed him on the mouth.

"Thank you," she said.

He could think of nothing to say. He let her out, and watched her go down the steps and fade away into the shadow of the willows.

It was very late when he came in. Phyllis was sitting up in bed, her knees drawn up tightly beneath the covers; she was brushing her hair.

"Where were you?" she asked.

He was already weary with her hurt and wonderment, before it had even come to pass. "I was in the mill," he said.

"In the dark?"

"In the dark."

"Doing what?"

"Sitting. Sitting and listening."

"Listening to what?"

"To the wheel," he said.

He put on his nightshirt while she watched him. He had a suspicion suddenly, with that intuition of spouses, that desire was waking in her as she looked upon him. And sure enough, when he put out the light and lay down in bed, she leaned close to him in a way that meant she longed for him.

But then she stopped. In the moonlight he could see by her expression that her mind was staggered.

"You smell like apples," she said. "Like apples and . . . like another woman."

4

For several weeks Colen denied even the existence of Cynthia to his wife. But the more he denied, the more hurt Phyllis became; for she knew that he had closed his heart to her behind a lie. How big or small the lie was, she did not know; but she could not be lied out of her certain knowledge that he had been with another woman on that night he had been late at the mill.

And the more he denied, the more fruitless became his denial, because he sickened himself with it. Finally he stopped responding at all to Phyllis's grieving and frustrated questions; and then she stopped asking them.

For a space her hurt seemed to ebb. He noticed that where she had been capable and thoughtful before, her concern that everything in the household meet his expectations redoubled. The house underwent a spring cleaning even though now the season was autumn. The dishes she set before him were his favorite, and perfectly cooked. The chores that might have been left to him melted away while he was in the mill. Her compulsion extended even to enforcing better behavior from the children, who had always been mannerly, but now regarded him with almost superstitious awe. She nearly coerced him into making love to her, as if to demonstrate her willingness to offer him everything.

Her efforts to win him back only worked against her. They disgusted him. They were a reproach. He thought of the vague helplessness of Cynthia, and lying awake, alone beside his wife, he dwelled on the few kisses Portius's wife had given him, while the love of his own marriage went untasted.

Preoccupation became obsession. He lived in a world of unreal events, of fantasies that in his morally lucid moments he found abhorrent—of trysts in the mill, of Cynthia appealing to him to run away with her, even of Portius dying and of Phyllis leaving him, leaving him free.

One day he came out of the racket of the mill and stood on the steps for a long while, thinking, dreaming bitter dreams. Winter was in the air. He felt again the closeness of the house, heard the quietness of his wife and the chatter of the children, foresaw the winter chores. He remembered the long battle with the snows, the cold that cut the fingertips, the light of day always waning. Against this, it seemed to him, he had only Cynthia; he thought of gathering her close and pressing his face into the fragrant hollow of her neck above her open bodice; and he desired her overwhelmingly.

He went away up the mountain road. He hardly knew what he was doing, except that he knew that when he found her he was going to ask her to go away with him. Where, he had not yet thought; it did not matter.

As he was approaching the steading he saw Portius driving his wagon and team out of the lane end. Colen stood stock still in the road, watching, and made no attempt to conceal himself; but Portius turned the wagon the other way on the main road and did not see him.

To Colen this seemed like the hand of God. He had not thought how he was going to speak to Cynthia alone; he had imagined that Portius was still confined to his bed. Evidently the man was up and about, although the crutch hooked over the seat of the wagon showed him still a cripple. Colen hurried on, suddenly elated, sure of his success.

She was making pies in the kitchen. The apple peelings were strewn everywhere underfoot; the child was eating them and a kitten in the corner was playing with them. He had expected the smell of the fruit, because he associated it with her, and it aroused him even more.

She had been crying, he saw, before her husband had left. When he looked in the door, which had been left open to vent the heat of the oven, and she caught sight of him, she put her apron hastily to her eyes, and rubbed the clinging dough from her fingers. She cast a glance over her child and then came toward him—looked at him a moment—and stepped outside, closing the door behind her.

"What are you doing here?" she asked. But she was not displeased.

He did not answer her—or at least, not aloud. But his look was so hungry and so urgent that she blushed.

"Come with me," she said. She took him by the wrist and tugged him toward the woodshed, looking around fearfully as she did so, as if expecting her husband to return at any moment.

Inside the shed, out of sight of anyone, she faced him. "So?" she asked.

He took her in his arms and kissed her. She kissed him back freely, even laughing softly under her breath in delight at his impetuousity. He sat down and pulled her onto his lap; she nuzzled him, breathing warmth onto his chilly neck. He undid the lacing of her bodice and set his hand on her breast; she helped him by pulling aside the cloth, and smiled at the liberty he took.

"Come away with me," he said.

She had been about to kiss him but stopped, puzzled. "What?"

"I said, Come away with me. Leave your husband. I'll leave my wife. We'll start over somewhere else. I'll build another mill—I'll be rich again, and you'll never be poor."

She giggled and rubbed his cheek playfully, as if in lieu of a slap to bring him back to his senses. "Don't talk nonsense," she said.

"I'm not," he insisted. But she seemed not to be paying attention.

"I missed you," she said sadly.

"I missed you, too. By God, Cynthia, I've thought of you every minute since the night you came to the mill."

"Did your wife guess about me?"

"Yes."

"I thought she would. Women always know. Men never guess. Not even Portius, with all his jealousy, ever could guess I'd be sitting here with you right now."

Colen groaned softly in impatience at the conversation. He put his hand up under her skirts and felt her buttocks: they were warm and round and smooth, smooth as an apple. She smiled and snuggled closer to him.

"Colen, Colen," she whispered. "What would I do without you?"

"You must come away with me. Now. Tonight. Whenever and as soon as you can."

"Don't be silly," she said, kissing him.

"I'm not being silly," he said, exasperated. "I mean it."

"What about my husband? I can't just leave my husband."

"Why not?"

"Because he's my husband. And you just can't run away from your wife. She's your wife. And what about your children, and Sissy?"

"Bring your daughter with you," he said. "My wife can get a man to run the mill. She's very capable," he added bitterly. "She doesn't need me, anyway. But I need you. And you need me. Don't argue with me, Cynthia. We don't have much time to plan. If you won't come now, this minute, tell me when to come for you."

She frowned. "I don't want to hear another word of this," she said. "I won't run away with you." Then she softened her tone and kissed him and smiled. "I like you. You mean a lot to me. But running away is madness; I won't do it. Portius will take care of me, and I have to take care of him. And he's Sissy's father. That's important."

Colen could scarcely believe what he was hearing. He had never expected this.

"What *you're* saying is madness," he retorted. "How can we live without each other?"

She smiled. "Who ever said we had to do that?" she said. She took his hand, which was now gripping her dress, and held it against her breast.

He grew angry. "What? Creep around, kissing and clutching each other, pretending we love others, when it's really ourselves we love? It would be awful! I couldn't do it."

She sat up straight and thrust his hand away. At that moment the door of the shed opened a crack and the little girl looked in.

Cynthia stood up. "Go back to the kitchen, Sissy. Mama will be right back." The child lingered at the door, watching them with forlorn, dark eyes, lost in astonishment at what big people did. Cynthia laced up her bodice determinedly and straightened her skirts.

Colen too was stunned. He leaned back against the wall of the shed, watching this woman in amazement. Never had he imagined that she might react this way, so irrationally, with such an incomprehensible mixture of morality and licentiousness. Or was he being irrational? And what had happened to his morality?

"I think you'd better go home," she said firmly.

Tears smarted at the edges of his eyes. She must have seen them there, because she suddenly reached out a hand and ran her fingers through his hair in a forgiving and fond caress.

But then she turned and left. He waited a moment and then rushed out after her. At the door of the house she paused, scooting the child before her into the kitchen. "Go on," she said to Colen. "Portius will be back soon. He just went down the road to the neighbor's. I've pies to bake. And I'm sure you have work to do."

"Will you think about it?" he implored her.

She smiled, kindly as before. "No," she said firmly. "And you shouldn't think about it either."

She went into the kitchen and closed the door behind her.

5

Phyllis, too, was baking pies when he returned. The irony of this struck him as he came in heavily and stood by the fire with his back to her, holding his hands out automatically to warm them. Here there were no peelings on the floor; the crusts were rolled and cut on the marble tabletop with nary a wayward crumb permitted. He glanced at her, as if looking to confirm his certainty that she would be, as always, controlled and quiet. She smiled at him cheerfully as she caught his eye; lately she had been seizing at every moment, hoping it would be the one when his affections began to return to her.

But once again, with her unsleeping intuition, she sensed that something had happened. She left her work and came close to him; she hesitated, looking into his eyes; and then, as if refusing to let him tell her a lie again, she seized him by the shirt and pressed her face against him, drawing in deep breaths—sniffing him, he realized, the way a dog sniffs its master when he has returned from a walk alone.

The apple smell, the woman smell must have been the same as on that other occasion. She burst into tears and clung to his shirt, hiding her face hopelessly against his chest. Then she went away and stood by the window. The last light of the autumn afternoon clearly showed the tears streaking her cheeks.

"You saw her again," she said.

"Yes, I did," he admitted. His confession, after so many denials, relieved him of none of his guilt.

She lifted her face like one harkening to a distant sound. "Who is she, Colen? For God's sake, tell me. Tell me whom my husband loves."

"Her name is Cynthia. She's Portius's wife, the man who brought the grain and then broke his leg. I swear to you, Phyllis, I've never lain with her."

"Maybe you have, maybe you haven't," she said. "But you love her. You would lie with her if you could.—What is it, Colen? Won't she have you? Dear man, have you thrown yourself away on a woman who doesn't love you?"

"She loves me well enough."

"Then why don't you go with her? If you love her, and she loves you, why don't you go away with her? Do you know what torture it is for me to lie beside you at night, and know that you're thinking of another woman, that you're lying with another woman in your thoughts? I love you, Colen. If you can be happy with her, go."

"She won't have me," he said. He began to weep again.

His wife was silent for a long time, startled and confused.

"Not have you?" she said finally, numbly. "Not have my Colen? Why not?"

"She says it wouldn't be right."

Phyllis sobbed sharply. "God bless her!" she cried. "And you, Colen, what do you think?"

He looked at her, haggard with his tears and his pain.

"Me?" he said. "I'd go with her. I'd go with her tomorrow. But what can I do? She won't have me."

"Oh, Colen! Colen!"

Phyllis sank into a chair and wept. There was no way that Colen could retract the truth he had uttered; and yet he could not bear, either, to hear her sobbing. So he went out again, heading for the mill.

As he staggered over that brief ground it occurred to him that Cynthia knew, even in the lightness of her fidelity, that to leave her husband would be wrong. Why, Colen wondered, did he himself not know the same?

It was true that in some abstract way he understood that what he had asked Cynthia to do was wrong, wrong to Portius and to Phyllis and all their children. And wrong to himself and to Cynthia, too.

But he would never question leaving with Cynthia, because somehow in the twisting and turning of his thoughts, it was yet right that he do it. For all his life, doing what was right had only depended upon his knowing what the right was. And his sense of what was right had always been strong—even now, in his wrongdoing, it did not absolutely fail him. And yet somehow, he thought, it would be right to do this wrong thing, and he would still do it if he could.

How had things become so upside-down, so confused? How had right and wrong become mixed up together so that each was part of the other? Was it only from listening to his own little exasperations and discontents for too long? It reminded him of the wheel, the gearwheel in the mill, that went round and round forever, this great wheel of human excuses, justifications, hopes, and devisings, which ground wrong into right and right into wrong.

He went into the mill and sat down beneath the clattering of the wheel, hoping it would drown out his confusion and his pain; but the noise only seemed a part of the great cacophony of his thoughts.

# Beneath the Sky

The saints are sinners who keep on trying.
—Robert Louis Stevenson

We gain the strength of the temptation we resist.
—Emerson

'Tis one thing to be tempted, Escalus,
Another thing to fall.

—Shakespeare

For a long time after Cory's wife left him, the hill was a hard place. It seemed that the path that climbed to his house there grew narrow; fewer feet beat upon it. He worked under the wide sky in the garden, or laying up stones that the frost had shaken off the long walls about the fields, and he was alone there in the sight of God, who lived in the cold sky, watching him.

But in time his new life took shape, rose up like a crystal growing, putting out sharp shards and spines that knit into a seamless, smooth enclosure as vast as a cathedral. He dwelt on the floors of the fields and God in the high ceiling, and yet they dwelt within one space together.

He felt, though, that it was hard to be alone with God. He felt his weaknesses intently. All the conflicting interests and passions of his life, which he had once cherished so proudly as proof of his wide knowledge and his sensitivity to all views, to everything human—these clashing appetites he now distrusted. He was a man of peace—why did a gun hang on his wall? He believed in the equality and dignity of women—why, beside the gun, did there hang that painting a traveling painter had made years ago, of a naked woman cowering before a raging man? And beside that painting, the shelves of books containing every species of human knowledge, after which he had hopelessly hungered when he was young. Now he searched for God's knowledge, knowing that the endless search for the world's knowledge is empty.

His wife had gone back to the world. She wanted to wear the world's bright clothing before she died, to travel in cities where she could see and be seen. She had gone to the huckster's booth, willing to sell herself into bondage, as long as she could join the carnival.

So Cory was alone, gradually coming to understand how he had been alone even before she left.

One evening music drifted to him as he was shutting the west gate. The sounds of the village rarely reached to the hill, but on this night a breeze was rising out of the sunset, lifting warm air up the land. Without another thought, in the great impulse of loneliness, he climbed over the gate (forgetting even that he could open it and walk through) and started down the path.

He was walking into the sunset. He did not take the cart track, but the shorter route, where the path twisted and turned over land too heaving and falling for any cart. After a time he came out on a stretch of the rolling earth where he could see well ahead of him. His neighbors were coming together out of their own fainter footpaths, falling in purposefully on the main way, intent on the music that called with increasing sweetness as he approached the village.

He saw Phyllis, too, come up the path from the mill by the river, with her trio of little ones orbiting around her, all three shrieking, laughing, complaining at once. She was the wife of Colen, a good man but a troubled. He did not treat her well. He had almost left her for another man's wife who lived beyond the mountain; and she carried the hurt still, hoping he would efface it with freely given love and a change of heart, but he could not. She had told Cory once that Colen would still go beyond the mountain if the other woman would have him.

Phyllis was one of the few who knew the truth of Cory's own troubles. She had listened; out of her own pain she had much to share. He felt he knew her well; and though he was almost frightened sometimes by the greatness of the hurt she cherished, he admired her for her fidelity. Many men and women flirted as a matter of course, meaning nothing by it; but Phyllis had never flirted with him, never suggested by any look or smile that she felt more than friendship toward him. It was rare that a man and a woman knew one another as well as did he and Phyllis, without any false flirtation. Or without a yearning outside fidelity.

The music came from a fiddler's bow, from the throat of a hand organ, and the rattling of the bones. The folk were already lining up for the dance when he came into the village square, which was lit with the light of torches and lanterns. He wandered around the margin of the crowd, saying hello to neighbors as he went. He would have asked what the occasion was, but he guessed it was no more than the coming of the musicians.

When the dancing began, he sat down on a bench and watched. And though he laughed, though he clapped his hands, beat his foot on the hardened dirt, and whooped to the dancers as they sashayed down the lines, he felt still more alone than he had on his hilltop.

But he thrust the feeling away. Here was Grey, a wiry man who shared Cory's plowing in some years, sashaying with his own youngster for a partner, his feet flying in all directions as if he meant to cut the most comical figure he could. Other farmers, bull-necked and thick-limbed, stomped broad boots in the dance; giggling girls and strident boys ran here and there in a holiday frenzy; and toddlers strutted about at the edges of their mothers' sight, beaming at their supposed independence.

And he began to notice the women as well. Here was Meggin, the young widow who lived down by the river, dancing with her new beau; Cora, who was there without her husband; Daphne, too; and of course Phyllis, whom he saw once dancing with Grey and once again with Meggin for a partner. There were several women with partners, yet without their husbands.

He knew them all well, and had for years. But he thought he had never noticed how tall Meggin stood, how straight and free she looked when she shook back her long flaxen braid and laughed. And Cora, how she glowed with happiness, quick and lively on her short legs; Daphne, turning to right and left, like a flame bursting up white and high above red embers.

And Phyllis. He thought he had never seen her before. She was so slender, so handsome, so graceful, it was an effort to take his eyes from her, and when he lost her in the throng, it was a troubled moment until she reappeared again.

One of Cora's little girls rushed up to him and urged him to dance. An adult he would have refused, but this little one he could not deny. Then, in the whirl of the circle, Phyllis came round before him, smiling brightly at finding him. The dance called for him to lean forward and clap his hands behind her head. Warmth, a faint scent of roses, and she was gone, laughing, as the circles turned one within the other.

He sat out for quite some time. His thoughts seemed to whirl like the dancers. Why were these other men's wives so attractive now? He knew and liked their husbands. The mere idea of seduction, of encouraging anyone in infidelity, could not possibly take root in his mind; and yet he looked on and yearned after each in turn as she whirled by.

A new dance was forming. The crowd parted accidentally before him and he saw Phyllis walking along its edge, coming in his direction, her eyes searching in the throng. She saw him, stopped, smiled, and beckoned to him with one finger in mock imperiousness. He rose. He felt it was a mistake, and yet he could not resist.

They danced to breathlessness, through arches of upraised arms, down snaking lines and around circles of clapping, laughing partners. He hardly knew what his feet did, but he knew his face hurt with a smile of delight. Shy he was, afraid to be clumsy, but conscious too of the touch of Phyllis' damp, warm hands in his own. He felt he held a ray, a dazzling light that was a woman.

Several times her children interrupted them, bursting upon the dance, shouting to be taken in, but then they left again, and the dance went on.

And stopped at last.

"Thank you for the dance," said Phyllis, looking at him and then away.

"Thank you for making me dance," he answered.

He left for home as the next round began. He saw her with Grey and was pleased she had a partner, pleased she had set aside her pain for the time.

He did not go down into the village for months. He stayed on the hill and minded his work as best he could; but Phyllis was in his thoughts, and he could not work her out of them.

He asked God what the meaning of it all was, and in the silence of the sky he heard his own answer and knew that answer was right: there was no meaning to it at all. He was in love with Phyllis, but he could not have her. "She has a ring on her finger," he said to himself. "That's the beginning and the end of it for you. That's all you have to know about her. That's all you have to think about her." And yet he thought much more than that about her, all the day; and at night he dreamed about her.

"If only," he caught himself saying one day, "if only Colen would leave her. If only he would go beyond the mountain to the woman he really prefers. If only that other man's wife would want Colen—then I could want Colen's wife." He forgot for a moment the cruelty of his wish; for to want a married woman is to play God. He thought how he would cherish her—how he would ease, with his unstinting love and his fidelity, the hurt of her.

"She's a pearl," he told himself. "And if you're walking down the road and you see a man ahead of you cast down a pearl he mistakes for a pebble, the pearl is yours. The pearl belongs to the man who knows its value. If he ever casts her away . . ."

Then the silence of this cathedral he had built of loneliness and sky mocked him gently. "Don't want things you're not to be given," he said to himself. He saw clearly all of a sudden that this love was another of those paradoxes of which he seemed to be formed, of wants that he knew were wrong.

His neighbors went so long without seeing him that at last they grew curious, even worried about his long absence. Though they could see the smoke above his chimney by day, still they thought he might be sick. One day Phyllis came up the path with a basket of things—herbs, some of her own bread, and the apple butter she made better than anyone.

"Cory!" she called, as she pushed through the west gate and closed it behind her. He looked up and saw her through the window of the shed, where he was sharpening a scythe. His heart felt like the heart of a hare when the hounds pass by the mouth of the burrow, sniffing. And yet he was not afraid of her; he was only afraid of himself, of his weakness.

He thought of hiding there in the shed. She would look in the house, scan the fields, and then go away, puzzled, maybe troubled, but he could be sure she would not find him.

"This is foolishness," he thought. "Be the man you are, Cory. God is here helping you do what's right; don't fear the longing in your heart. God won't let it turn evil."

So he went to the door, raised his arm, and called cheerfully to her.

She came over the field, radiant, smiling with the pleasure of beholding him. He saw her slenderness and felt a twinge of fear again. "How nice to see you well," she said. "We've been imagining all sorts of things about you. I couldn't stand wondering anymore—I had to come up and see you for myself."

"I'm fine," he said. "I thank you all for your concern. I admit I've been at fault for it; I've been hiding up here."

"Doing what?" she asked, smiling.

"Talking with God," he answered.

"Then I have no cause to pity you," she said. "I thought maybe you were feeling lonely."

"There's loneliness and there's loneliness. I don't think God intended I should live alone without human company. But then again I'm only just learning to listen to God's intentions for me, so maybe I've judged wrong."

"No, I'm sure God meant you to have a wife," she said simply. "God wouldn't leave so fine a man as you without a helpmeet."

There was no deeper meaning hidden in her words. She spoke the plain truth of her thoughts. He relaxed somewhat, thinking how much easier her fidelity made his task.

"Would you like some tea? The fire is still astir."

"I'd be glad to join you. Let's have some of the mint I brought."

He led the way into the house and busied himself with the fire and the kettle. She stood by, answering his queries about Colen and the children, about her bees and the goats she kept. Constantly she looked for ways to help him, fetching the cups out of the cupboard, warming the teapot, and spooning in the herbs. This helpfulness and readiness he knew in her from before and almost reveled in it. His wife had been content to let him do all.

She sat by the stove, and he at some distance away. He meant not to trust himself any more than he had to. They talked—he hardly knew of what—of pleasant things, of the children and of the plants that came up from the earth. He was only conscious that the time was passing, that she was there before him, kind, beautiful, simple, hurt—and that he was mastering his emotion, outwaiting it, that soon she would rise to leave and they would say their farewells and they would both be safe again. Safe in their loneliness.

"So, Cory," she said finally, "Tell me truly: How are you doing without a wife?"

He was surprised that she had reverted to the topic, and shifted uneasily in his chair, without an answer.

"I'm sorry," she said, suddenly sad. "I didn't mean to pain you."

He found he could not speak for a minute.

"I'll do well," he said. "Just not yet. I've a ways to go before I'm quite comfortable, I guess. Sometimes I think I'm doing well, and then I find myself . . . yearning. I suppose that's the word I'd use, but it's almost a crazy kind of hunger, for the sweet things that go with marriage."

"I know," she said softly.

They sat for quite some time in silence.

"I'd better go," she said. "A bear pushed over one of the skeps, and I've got to do something about it before nightfall." That mundane detail seemed to give him strength.

"Yes," he said, rising, "I've got a little mowing to do."

She went to the door. He stayed where he was, watching her, heartsick. She paused, turned, looked back at him.

"How about a hug for me, Cory?" she asked.

This had been a custom with them. When she had listened to him after his wife left him, she had consoled him in parting with a sisterly and chaste embrace.

He felt that it would just be a moment, just one more moment of restraint and he would be clear. He could trust himself for just one moment.

He went to her where she stood by the door. She leaned forward and put her arms around him, as if determined to prove something. Only their upper bodies touched.

Then suddenly they were clinging to each other, and suddenly they were kissing one another deeply and hungrily.

He drew back, took her hands gently from his shoulders, and pushed them away. She leaned against the doorpost. Her face was flushed as brightly as when they had danced, but her eyes were confused, happy but hurt at the same time, trying not to look at him, but failing.

"I'd better go," she whispered hoarsely.

"No. Wait. Not yet." He put his hand on the door as if to bar her way, but then he backed away, leaving her free to go if she wished.

But she did not so wish. He realized suddenly that she loved him as he loved her, in a kind of blind, ignorant, hopeful infatuation.

"I fell in love with you about three months ago," he said. She raised her head. He could tell that for her it had been much longer.

"You're so . . ." he began, hesitating. "Beautiful. Fine. I think that if I could have you to love I could give up the old things that aren't right with me, that don't make sense in my life anymore."

She was trembling and weeping. "If we could be together . . ." she murmured.

"But we can't," he said. "We're like two children who have found out they can't resist the honeycomb. It's got to be put away, out of reach, high on a shelf."

"Who's going to put it there?" she asked.

"God will."

She nodded, looking away.

After a minute she put her hand on the latch.

"Just one thing I want you to promise me," he said. She looked at him.

"I want you to promise me you'll never apologize for that. For that embrace. You'll never say you're sorry. Because I'm not. I'll always remember it, I'll always be glad of it."

She nodded again. "I promise," she said, in a whisper.

They looked one last time into one another's eyes. Then she went out the door.

He waited until she was away from the house before he went to the window that looked out on the west. There he could see her going home. At first she walked with a heavy step, as if she were carrying a weight that had not been there when she came. But as she went, she looked up at the sky, and her stride became lighter, freer. By the gate she turned and looked back for a moment. That act had something of gratitude in it, though Cory felt that no thanks belonged to him.

When she was quite gone he took the gun down from the wall and broke it. Then he cut the painting out of its frame and thrust it into the stove to burn. The books he left; they would do no harm if he never opened them.

Then he went outside again. The sky was wide and silent.

# The Lord's Well

All my springs are in thee.

—Psalms 87:7

He that believeth in me, out of the inmost hollow of his being shall flow streams of living water.

—John 7:38

Life is a gamble, or so people say. If so, I have certainly bought my share of figurative lottery tickets, and even a few literal. That is exactly why I object to gambling: I know what it is to be distracted from actually learning to live in the life one has made for oneself—or from finding a way to truly escape from it—by the hope that one will be magically rescued by good luck.

How easy it is to see this distraction in oneself, to detest it; and yet to buy and buy again in the lottery of life, living on the drug of deluded hope. And how easy to learn this lesson in one part of one's life, and yet fail to apply the lesson to other, more fundamental forms of self-delusion and distraction. The trapped wife hoping that her abusive husband will be killed in a traffic accident; the student hoping his classmates will be called on first; the writer thinking his bills will be paid at last if only he sells that book in his drawer—these are all small or large buyers in the lotteries of existence.

But I am speaking of myself. I have attempted to sell my books to hundreds of publishers and agents over a period of twenty-five years. Very early in the process I became numb to rejection; and as I became more savvy about the publishing business, I began to see that publishers had very cogent reasons for rejecting what I wrote. Lists fill up; tastes vary; higher-ups in the corporate structure are demanding sure sellers, books utterly unlike mine. I quickly lost that narcissistic certainty, so common in young writers, that the world somehow owed me publication. I even began to wonder if I really wanted to publish on the industry's terms.

Yet even as I came to this point of view, I continued to believe that publication would lift me into a life in which I could read and write and think as productively as possible—in which I could be most useful to my fellow humans. Although I started out with more selfish interests, gradually that became the goal that I sought: the life lived to the maximum of one's talent in the service of others. And I do not think this is a sugarcoating on a selfish hope. For if you consider it, what other reason is there for living? Our past, such as we understand it, teaches us that we are young creatures; our future, if the example of other species is applicable, is eventual extinction. We construct vast edifices of religious belief on hearsay, on promises that remain unfulfilled for millennia, on denial of the flesh or on hopes for the spirit; and yet all we really have, when the dogmas and delusions are stripped away, is one another: in our fellow humans and in our fellow creatures on earth lies our only sure source of meaning. It has been said that loving god and loving one's neighbor are everything; indeed, they are the very same thing. Whatever god is, it speaks most unmistakably in our love for one another and our earth—this love cannot lie, however prophets and preachers may.

Thus in middle life I found myself in a dilemma: I understood that my work would never be published, and yet I believed that without publication I would never be useful; and if I were never useful, my life would never truly have meaning.

How I resolved this difficulty requires a parable.


I began building my house when I had no money.

I had no work and nothing else to do. I had bought an acre and a half of grown-over farm with the proceeds of the sale of the house and fifty acres of my vanished marriage; for hills and fields and ponds and streams now I had a pinched parallelogram of land crowded by a road.

Little, but mine. As I cut back the jagged hawthorn and the spidery alder, I found an old driveway. It led to an equally old cellarhole, formed of walls now buckled by frost and rain, taken over by red willow and fire cherry and poplar. The farmhouse had burned in the big fire that tore through Trescott in '57; in the rubble of its chimney were old bottles melted into smeared globules of glass.

It was spring when I began my labor. I worked in a tide of birdsong and fragrance. On all sides the birds were nesting; then the shadberry and the wild cherry bloomed, then the hawthorn, and last the old apple trees. I cut carefully, respectfully, taking no more than I had to; and the land emerged from its disguise.

I hauled the rocks from the cellarhole, rolling by way of a ramp those I could not carry; back-cracking work, but my labor was free, and I worked with joy, because I was building my own house.

The more time I spent on the land, the more my eye picked out features of the old farm disguised by change: here there had been a shed—I found its outline in grassy stones, even its mossy roofbeam. A ditch had run to the road to drain the hardpan. A pattern emerged in the trees—apples along the western line; and in what once had been a dooryard was a stand of lilacs now twenty feet across. And in the back, at the lowest point of the property, was a depression in the earth, filled with water all spring. It seemed to me the remnant of an old well.

Summer came. I had work again, and a little money. I drew plan after plan, gradually reinventing one of the most economical forms of housing, the cape; and while I debated costs and results with myself, I called in a contractor to dig for water.

Curtis was a sharp old Yankee; he was not sure that I was right about the well. "Lowest point on the property," I said, "and see the trench that leads from there back to the house? They must have had a water line there." He rubbed his grizzled chin dubiously, but allowed himself convinced enough to try.

He brought in three well tiles—concrete cylinders three feet in diameter and four feet in height. This would give me a total well depth of ten feet or so, allowing for clearance at the top; the well would hold about 70 cubic feet of water, over 500 gallons. I could almost smell that water already, the sweet coolness of it.

With hired help standing by and a truckload of gravel ready to bed the tiles, Curtis ran his backhoe down to the site, set up, and began digging. Within a minute he had cut into clay as dry as the ash in the belly of a stove; into clay that had lain sealed from water and undisturbed since the glaciers had sloughed it off in their slow retreat ten thousand years ago.

He dug down as far as his backhoe would reach, and the hole grew (if possible) only drier and drier.

"Stuart," he said, "I think we're diggin' into the backside of the Sahara."

I had to admit he was right. There was no well here, and there never had been one.

He refilled the hole. In a few weeks he managed to sell the well tiles to another customer. "If you ever find where that old well was," he said, "give me a call."

I looked everywhere on that piece of land. I poked in every thicket; I crawled through the lilacs; I jabbed and banged with shovel and crowbar. I called the previous owner; she was long gone, living cozily in an apartment in Massachusetts. The land had been her husband's; she had never lived on it. She spun me a hopeful story about how the well was "somewhere out in front of the house." Certainly she was wrong; a well would not completely disappear in a mere thirty years of disuse.

One day I was driving back from Machias and saw Saul on the road, riding his bicycle home from a visit to a friend. I pulled over and told him my problem with the well.

"What you should look for," he said, "is a pile of rocks. That's the way my well was when I found it. I had no idea it was a well; I was just doing something up there one day and noticed a little dampness by one of the rocks in a pile, so I pulled it out. There was more water under it, so I pulled another out. And I just kept going—you've seen my well."

Saul's well was about fifteen feet deep, about four feet across, lined with stone all the way down. It was hard to imagine that it had ever been caved in, a sunken heap of rocks.

I went straight back to the land and wandered around it one more time in the soft, rich light of the Maine summer evening. I felt sure that this time I could find it, now that I knew what to look for; and I prayed to god for a leading to the right place.

And in a few minutes, on the back edge of another slope, not far from where the shed had been, I came across a sunken heap of half-buried rocks.

I took a shovel and a bar and began to dig. Beneath one rock was another, and another; and they were loose as if they had toppled inward, fallen together; no dirt had washed into their interstices over centuries. Someone had moved these rocks here at some time, however they might now be disordered and displaced.

As I pulled out the rocks, I praised god. A homestead without water is a useless place; here was god's well, an answer to a prayer.

But at about two feet down I hit dry clay, lots of it, hard and tight and obviously undisturbed by human activity. This was no well; this was only a heap of rocks some farmer had dragged out of a field and thrown carelessly into a depression in the earth. So much for my prayers—or at least, so much for my expected answer to them.

During that summer I finally located an old-timer who confirmed what I feared. There was no well on the property. The land had been more extensive once; now it was parcelled up. The neighbors owned the spot where the well had been.

In October I called in a well driller, a man named Lord who had been in the business so long everyone had a story about him. I figured I could pay him at most about two thousand dollars. He would charge eight dollars per foot of depth for a hole six inches in diameter. Between the surface and bedrock he would have to install a steel well casing at a cost of ten dollars a foot. Thus until he hit bedrock he would be spending my money at the rate of eighteen dollars per foot.

The rig truck was a monster. He backed it up the ancient driveway, which was now muddy with fall rains, and almost rolled the truck over when one wheel sank in the ditch. We worked to extricate the rig, piling cordwood under the hydraulic stabilizers. For an hour or more our efforts were fruitless, but the driller remained sanguine. "It ain't stuck until all four wheels are pointin' straight up," he said.

When finally freed, positioned, stabilized, with its drilling tower swung into the sky, the rig seemed to dwarf us. Its engine blotted out every other sound for a half mile; its bit whirled and plunged into dirt and clay, grinding money to pieces as it went. And the clay was deep: the drill sank to forty-two feet before it hit bedrock. I spent nearly eight hundred dollars just to reach the point where we could search for water. Several more hours were consumed in setting the casing, as yards and yards of clay turned to soup around the bit, but finally powdered gray rock began to churn up over the top of the pipe.

As the crew drilled, they checked periodically for water. At 180 feet I ran out of money, the sky was almost dark, and the well was still dry.

"We can't just pull up the drill and quit," said Lord.

"I can't pay you any more," I said.

"What are you going to do? You got to have a well, don't you?"

"You'll have to come back some time when I have the money."

"And center over this hole again? It'd be just about impossible. You saw all the trouble we had getting in here the first time. Look, we're here, we've got the drill centered—you can owe us for the rest."

I disliked that idea right away.

"I'll tell you what," he said. "You think about it overnight. We'll leave the rig right here. Sometimes during the night the water will break in from a seam, and the well will be full when you come back in the morning."

I said okay. We left the man-dwarfing, sky-looming, earth-piercing rig in place, its money-burning engine silent for the night.

At six-thirty next morning we met again on the frozen ruts of the driveway. The driller took a small stone and held it over the wellhead. "Listen to it fall," he said. "If it hits water right away, we'll know the well is full." He let the pebble loose and it fell and fell and fell and fell. It fell for what seemed like a minute, like several minutes. Finally it splashed into water that seemed unimaginably distant.

"Wow," he said. "That's *way* down there."

He fired up the drill and lowered the bit, like a big dipstick, a hundred and eighty feet into the earth; then he pulled it up. The last five feet were wet.

"Not much water, considering it's had all night to collect," he said.

I had made up my mind for better or worse during the night.

"Keep drilling," I told him.

While the drill roared I went out and sat in my car to get away from the sound. I could see the shank of the drill sinking by the second into the casing; I could count the dollars in feet and the feet in dollars. I had none of this money; this was all debt now, which I had done my best to avoid throughout the divorce disaster, with mixed success. I closed my eyes.

It all seemed wrong, the roaring machine, the debt, even the concept of piercing the earth to bring up the water nature had hidden away in the rock. That water was hidden away there for a reason; it seemed we should not be taking it.

But as I opened my eyes and raised my head to watch the rig again, I noticed the sign mounted on the spine of the drilling truck, spelled out in letters a foot high:

LORD'S WELL DRILLING

And in that ludicrous moment it struck me that the answer to my prayers had come in a different form from the one I had expected. I had wanted to find the easy well; I had expected god to provide it. This well would be harder; I would have to work for it, pay for it for years. But it was the only well god was going to give me. This well was the reality, and reality rules; reality defines the answer to prayer, not denial, delusion, expectation.

At 360 feet I told the driller to stop. The well was still dry, but I ordered a hydrofracture, a process by which the well is pressurized in the hope of breaking open seams that may have glazed over during the drilling. The procedure alone would cost $500, but it seemed to me that the well was deep enough to yield water if it was ever going to do so.

It proved the right decision. After the hydrofracture, water surged into the well and rose to within a dozen feet of the surface. The preliminary test showed the output at better than three gallons a minute; ultimately the well produced better than eight per minute.

Years went by after I had the well drilled. I built a cabin in which to live, but it was cramped, and I was lonely there. I moved about restlessly, sometimes staying on my land, sometimes renting elsewhere; for several years I left the state altogether. Building a true house began to seem an impossibility, a dream I had had before I learned the cold facts of time and money. Mr. Lord's well, finally paid for but disused beside the unkempt driveway, became no more than a reproach for my failure.

Finally I compromised with the time remaining to me: I had a house built, a little cape. It was trim, sunny, comfortable; it worked. For the first time in years I felt my soul's root dare to stretch into soil again.

And when the well was connected to the house, the water began to flow; tinged with reddish brown, gradually it grew clearer and clearer, useful at last.

That is the parable. This is the application:

It was around the time that I built the house that I began to understand that my work would probably never be published. And I began to come to terms with that eventuality as I never had before.

When I had gone looking for water, I had been looking for the well—my well—where I wanted it to be. I wanted it to be convenient, cheap, in fact already dug out by someone else. But there was no well where I was looking. No amount of looking, of expectation, could make my well appear there.

The well—the real well, god's well—was elsewhere. It was costly; its price in labor and uncertainty was high.

In the same way, all my life I had been expecting the world to discover it had a use for my writing. I expected that this discovery would become a wellspring in my own life that would allow me to do the kind of work I best loved and to live the way I most wanted to live.

But the world never found a use for what I wrote. I was looking for a well that was not there.

The real wellspring of my life was elsewhere, costlier in labor and in uncertainty; more difficult to rely on, because faith in it had to come not from outside me, but from within.

Every writer—for all I know, every artist—is told at some point that he should be doing his creative work for its own sake, and should care nothing whether it brings him fame or not. He is told that the sheer joy of creative writing should be enough for him. Of course he knows this already. The joy of the creative act has impelled him perfectly well, has been in fact his only reward, and he does not need to be reminded of its power. So the advice will be irritating; all the more so because he usually hears it from someone who has never created anything, or from someone who has the power to present his work to the public and has no intention of doing so.

But that rush of creative pleasure really is not enough in itself. An Artist (since I have ventured into discussing Art, I will push on with a capital *A*) should proceed through at least three stages in his career. The first is that in which he is driven by the simple, even self-centered and self-indulgent pleasure of creating something. In my case that first stage lasted for decades; but I finally broke through it to the second stage, in which I wanted my creative work to be of use to others. That is, I wanted what I wrote to help people be more compassionate; to help them understand their own humanity and that of others; to help them comprehend their vitality and mortality; to help them experience divinity.

This is not as hubristic as it sounds. Abraham Lincoln once commented of a certain man that god had for some unknown reason made him the worst of scoundrels, and yet also in his infinite wisdom had fortunately made him the worst of fools. The Artist, while he may well be a hubristic scoundrel, is also god's fool. I have never thought that I knew more, or had more experience, than others—that I had gained any extraordinary qualifications to teach or help others in life; but in mirroring life in what I created, I hoped to give people a glimpse of that thing that is the most difficult for us all to see, the workings of our own hearts.

Some never reach that second stage. One hears these writers interviewing themselves on the radio, boasting to us how they "live for the creative rush" that comes at the end of each novel. They seem not so much artists as drug addicts. Others who have progressed to the second stage fall back into the first when they find that the world will, after all, pay them for puerile, self-indulgent creative work.

But what of that other class, exemplified by the writer who never finds fame, but in midlife begins to realize that his work will never be known—that he will never help others simply because no one else will ever read what he writes? (That is the very moment when he is most likely to receive the advice that he should "write for himself," which is now triply unpalatable because he has finally progressed beyond self-indulgence.) Such a writer can publish his own work, as I publish this here, in the hope that his friends may profit from what he has to say; but in time he must move on to the next stage.

And that stage—that third stage—he reaches when he discovers that the creative act, aside from any usefulness to others, is one way of holding conversation with divinity. Whether he writes with indignation or a lover's passion, whether he writes to the Lord or the Higher Power or the Goddess, in his writing, in his conversation with god, in his telling of the human tale, he not only feels his own humanity more deeply, but feels as well how he is a part of divinity.

And for such a writer then, suddenly, there is a well in his life, though dug at cost; and there is water in the well, infinite springs of it; and though the water is so cold that it hurts his cupped hands as he holds them in the surging flow, still it is sweet, and his thirst grows as he drinks.

# Afterword

# A Plea

## for

# Self-Publication

A Speech
Delivered at the Home of Paul Swanson and Stefani Thrall
in Brooklin, Maine,
on the Occasion of the Publication of *Tales of Arcadia,*
July 8, 2000

My talk tonight begins with an epigraph from Robert
Louis Stevenson. I beg your indulgence for its length.

Poor soul, here for so little, cast among so many hardships, filled
with desires so incommensurate and so inconsistent, savagely
surrounded, savagely descended, irremediably condemned to prey
upon his fellow lives: who should have blamed him had he been of
a piece with his destiny and [been] a being merely barbarous? And
we look and behold him instead filled with imperfect virtues: . . .
sitting down, amidst his momentary life, to debate of Right and
Wrong and the attributes of the Deity. . . . To touch the heart of
his mystery, we find in him . . . the thought of Duty; the thought
of something owing to himself, to his neighbour, to his God: an
ideal of decency, to which he would rise if it were possible; a limit
of shame, below which, if it be possible, he will not stoop. . . . It
matters not where we look, under what climate we observe him, in
what stage of society, in what depth of ignorance, burthened with
what erroneous morality; by camp-fires in Assiniboia, the snow
powdering his shoulders, the wind plucking his blanket, as he sits,

passing the ceremonial calumet and uttering his grave opinions like a Roman senator; in ships at sea, a man inured to hardships and vile pleasures; . . . in the slums of cities, moving among indifferent millions to mechanical employments, . . . a fool, a thief, the comrade of thieves, even here keeping the point of honour and the touch of pity, often repaying the world's scorn with service, often standing firm upon a scruple, and at a certain cost rejecting riches:—everywhere some virtue cherished or affected, everywhere some decency of thought and carriage, everywhere the ensign of man's ineffectual goodness:—ah! if I could show you this! if I could show you these men and women, all the world over, in every stage of history, under every abuse of error, under every circumstance of failure, without hope, without help, without thanks, still obscurely fighting the lost fight of virtue, still clinging, in the brothel or on the scaffold, to some rag of honour, the poor jewel of their souls! They may seek to escape, and yet they cannot; it is not alone their privilege and glory, but their doom; they are condemned to some nobility; all their lives long, the desire of good is at their heels, the implacable hunter. . . .

—Pulvis et Umbra

My friends, you are very kind to gather like this to observe the launching of my little book. It is much too small, much too minor a book to deserve your attention; but I hope that you will be repaid for the considerable time you have spent driving here, and the dislocation of your normal schedules, by the superb hospitality of Paul and Stefani, and will look upon the publication of *Tales of Arcadia* as a useful excuse to enjoy summer on the Maine coast and the company of friends.

I cannot emphasize enough the minor nature of this book. Several people have said to me, "You must be proud of it"; but I am rather the reverse, and glad of being so. In order to write, in order to pursue any interest of one's own without the attention and support of the world, one has to cultivate a kind of arrogant certainty that one is doing something grand. This is the very attitude described by the great English novelist Charlotte Brontë:

> It is well that the true poet, quiet externally though he may be, has often a truculent spirit under his placidity, and is full of shrewdness in his meekness, and can measure the whole stature of those who look down on him, and correctly ascertain the weight and value of the pursuits they disdain him for not having followed. It is happy that he can have his own bliss, his own society with his great friend and goddess, Nature, quite independent of those who find little pleasure in him, and in whom he finds no pleasure at all. It is just, that while the world and circumstances often turn a dark, cold side to him—and properly, too, because he first turns a dark, cold, careless side to them—he should be able to maintain a festal brightness and cherishing glow in his bosom, which makes all bright and genial for him, while strangers, perhaps, deem his existence a Polar winter never gladdened by the sun. The true poet is not one whit to be pitied, and he is apt to laugh in his sleeve, when any misguided sympathizer whines over his wrongs. Even when utilitarians sit in judgment on him, and pronounce him and his art useless, he hears the sentence with such a hard derision, such a broad, deep, comprehensive, and merciless contempt of the unhappy Pharisees who pronounce it, that he is rather to be chidden than condoled with. (*Shirley*, chapter 4)

In publishing *Tales of Arcadia,* I finally have a chance to step back from that self-reinforcing stance. My greatest pleasure in publication is not that I finally have a book to be proud of, but that I finally have a book to be humble about.

The fact is that I think most of you will not like this book. I have said this to some of you individually, and have been met with indignant protests. But believe me, I know what I'm talking about. Dozens of times over the years people have asked to see something or other I've written, and I have given whatever it was to them, against my intuition or better judgment. And sure enough, by yielding to their insistence, I put them in the unpleasant position of either having to read something that did not suit their taste, or trying to avoid reading it without my finding out that they were neglecting it. The fact is that our tastes in reading generally differ; and if they do intersect at times, it is not necessarily where I happen to write. It would be interesting to do a Venn diagram of the types of books preferred by people in this room; it would be quite complex.

So I am not asking you to like this book; I'm not even asking you to read it. I do believe—I do know—that there are people out there in the world who will like this book, and to whom this book will mean a great deal; and if you yourselves know of any of them, I would appreciate your steering the book in their direction. My hope is that each of these copies will be passed from hand to hand, not buried at the bottom of a pile of books that a friend intends to read someday. That is why I am giving the majority of the 140 copies I have to libraries, and that is, in part, why none of the books is for sale. If a book has cost you nothing, you are much more likely to pass it along, or in this case to send it back to me so that I can do so. I intend to include with each of the books I give to individuals a card asking them to turn it over to someone else or to return it to me, when they decide they are finished with it one way or the other.

So what is this little book, anyway?

*Tales of Arcadia* is a collection of twelve stories and two essays, or rather I should say, one essay, twelve stories, and a concluding essay, with a page-long preface. I had not written a short story for well over twenty years when I sat down to write the first of these; in fact, I had written only one other short story before, excluding writing exercises in my childhood. I prefer longer fiction—very long fiction in fact, as I find more interest in developing characters and situations at length. My first novel, a short one, was about 70,000 words, about 170 printed pages; my second was about 500,000 words, or over 1200 pages; and the rest have fallen in between. I mention my inexperience with short fiction not to magnify my accomplishment as a neophyte in this field, but to excuse the book's deficiencies. I really don't know what I am doing when I take on the short story. Writing short fiction is very much à la mode, as I'm sure you know. Millions of writers across the land are cranking out short stories as I speak, flooding the editorial offices of the *New Yorker* with their wares, and hoping to get collections printed by all the major publishers, who are weary of thrusting them away. Writing schools thrive, from Maine to Iowa and beyond, on teaching "the craft of the short story." I have never attended such a school, and I fear their teachers and attendees would laugh at the ineptitude of my fictional devices; so I hope that if you do read these stories, you will be merciful.

The tales themselves, although in a fashionable genre, are very unfashionable in content. They are of a type called in French the *contes moraux,* moral tales. Obviously, I am talking about a story that teaches a simple moral lesson or a lesson about how to live life. These tales work by placing a character in a situation in which his or her morality and values are challenged, and examining the outcome. In their emphasis on morals and on our interaction with the divine, they are very outdated. I had a girlfriend once, briefly, who was *au courant* with the trends in fiction; though she praised the stories highly, she observed that they would never sell: not only because they were not set in modern times, but because they were, as she put it—and I have to quote her, because the expression she chose reveals all too well the attitude of the modern reader—"too God-y."

Well, perhaps they are too "God-y." My understanding of, or at least my thoughts about, divinity have changed enormously in the past ten years. And I did write these stories ten years ago, after all. The gap between writing and publication often produces an unbridgeable divide—this is one reason why people often don't publish their own work: they outgrow it too fast. When I consider how old the stories seem to me, I am reminded of the fact that when we survey the night sky, we are looking far, far back into time, unimaginably far back into time, inasmuch as the light of the stars we see with the naked eye has been dispatched anywhere from years to millions of years ago. This book is like the starlight of my past, a moment of my personal growth twinkling dimly in the present time. Although it is past, I am grateful that it has become so. *Tales of Arcadia* helped me grow; if it had not, it would have been useless to me and useless to anyone else.

In thanking you for your participation here today, I want to take note of the fact that by contrast with all of you, the world in general looks upon self-publication as the mark—the brand—of failure. If that is true, then this book is a failure. But I do not agree with the world, though it was not long ago that I did, or at least on this point. In this culture we imbibe this belief about publication from our early years on, whether we know it or not. A book, we are led to believe, is something that makes money, preferably a lot of money. Whenever I am asked about my profession and people learn that I am a writer, their next question is, "Published?"—a question usually delivered with a monetary gleam in the eye. If I have mentioned novels or fiction, the gleam is even harder and more calculating.

I am sick to my soul of that gleam. I feel as a person might who, after being praised for his or her good looks, is then asked, "Made any money with that body yet?" The ordinary person rigidly and unthinkingly equates success in the writing of a book with dollars in the bank. In the case of my book, I find I have to make repeated and tedious explanations as to why I am not selling it. People find this utterly baffling, as if I were giving away cash for nothing. The subject of money arises almost instantly when I describe what I have done.

Yet this attitude, this distortion of our understanding about what books are, is of fairly recent origin. Homer sang for his supper, true; but Homer never expected to become a millionaire. It was not really until the early 1800s that authors began to realize considerable wealth through the writing of fiction; and it was not until the early 1900s that the definition of the successful fiction writer as a wealthy person had completely taken hold, as far as I can tell.

Think of the best books you know, in fiction and nonfiction. Did they make their writers rich? I'll bet that on a list of fifty good writers, you might find one or two who became wealthy because of their work, and far more who died in wretched circumstances or who never dreamed of supporting themselves with something the world sets so little commercial value on as good ideas well expressed.

Think, too, of the richest writers you know. What is their writing like? Enough said.

Consider how this idiotic and wrong equation of success in writing with the making of money cripples writers today. First of all, it cripples them in the act of writing—they write to make money, many of them. To vary the analogy I have already used, this is like making love to make money. Not quite the same as doing it for free. I don't mean to pretend that I would *never* sign with a publisher and put my earnings to good use, but I would only do so under stringent conditions set by me—and in any case, I did not write these stories with that intent. Secondly, the distorted equation of writing and money-making cripples writers by persuading them that they are failures if they can't find a publisher. They never attempt to judge for themselves the intrinsic value of what they have created; instead they turn to others to do so.

And who are those others? Well, they are people who live in New York City, most of them. I could probably add another "Enough said" and leave it at that, but perhaps it would be more kind to point out that the Venn circles of editors in New York may not precisely coincide with the Venn circles of writers in Maine or Wyoming or Texas or California. Someone once badgered me in a vain attempt to get me to send one of these tales to the *New Yorker*. What an absurd idea! I might just as well have put it in a rocket and fired it off to Mars hoping for publication. The values reflected on these pages are utterly alien to the average urban sophisticate.

But maybe I am being prejudiced and provincial. Let me take another tack. Publishing today is a huge business. The little houses have in most cases been swallowed up by the big houses, and the big houses have been eaten up by the multimedia outfits. The little bosses in the publishing houses receive directives that tell them how much they are expected to produce, and with what financial resources. You may not realize this, but selling books is a lot like selling groceries—the profit margin can be pennies per book, though that is not true in every case. But it is true that in order to make decent profits, the publishers have to sell thousands upon thousands of copies. Each individual manager and editor knows that he or she must justify his or her continued presence on the payroll by bringing in money for the parent company. Survival requires finding the books that will sell the most, and spending all the allotted resources producing and marketing them. There simply is no room on the house list for *Tales of Arcadia* or anything like it. You wouldn't go to General Motors to ask them to sell the custom dune buggy you built yourself in your garage; don't go to the New York publishers to ask them to sell your book of short stories. The folks in the publishing houses are just trying to make a living, after all, just like the rest of us in our own jobs. It's a discourtesy, in a sense, to get in their way.

The effect of this system, however, is that writers internalize nonpublication as artistic failure; and they equate artistic failure with the failure of their entire lives. Their lives, they think, just don't add up—their training, their toil, their care, their love for their work—good for nothing but repeated rejection letters, and ultimately the dreaded drawer.

But I would ask them this: If life doesn't add up, who is doing the computation? Someone in New York? Why let those strangers sum up your life and your artistic work for you? If your work has value, if you really believe in it, publish it yourself. Give it away, or if you can't afford that, recoup your costs, but don't scheme to become a millionaire.

I want not only to dispel whatever doubts about self-publication may be lingering in this room, I want to go further and suggest that self-publication is a great action, even if the book is, as mine is, only a minor production. Self-publication is an act worthy of heroes; and we can become heroes, in our own hearts, if we give what we have to the world.

Let me describe an epiphany I had recently. (An epiphany is *de rigeur* in every lecture of this type.) I was recently in Harvard Square and spent several hours in the bookstores, tasting tidbits from the great banquet, the great feast of ideas we humans have had over the past two thousand years or so, in art, literature, mathematics, science, and other disciplines. When I had spent as much money on books as I could possibly rationalize or excuse, I went and sat in a sidewalk cafe looking out on the square.

I recommend the experience if you are looking for an epiphany. As a matter of fact, one of my favorite descriptions of epiphany is this passage from Yeats's poem "Vacillation":

> My fiftieth year had come and gone,
> I sat, a solitary man,
> In a crowded London shop,
> An open book and empty cup
> On the marble table-top.
>
> While on the shop and street I gazed
> My body of a sudden blazed;
> And twenty minutes more or less
> It seemed, so great my happiness,
> That I was blessèd and could bless.

A stack of great books on the table by your elbow, something chocolate to eat, something hot to drink; the great swarm of beautiful and intelligent people that buzz through Harvard University like killer bees; the warm sunshine—if that won't get you an epiphany, nothing will.

And the epiphany I had was that it is not just the love we have for one another that makes us great as human beings, a notion that has always been a truism for me; it is our ideas that make us great. Not just the good ideas, the E=mc²'s and the *Hamlets* and the Fermat's Last Theorems and the *Pietas,* but also the minor ideas, the half-baked ones, the flimsy ones; even they make us great as a species, simply because we have them.

If my epiphany doesn't seem all that persuasive, try it sometime in Harvard Square under the described circumstances.

Or just accept for the sake of argument that it is true. Then it is clear that we can join the human race, we can achieve our humanity, not only by loving one another, as in Christ's great commandment that we love our neighbor, but simply in having an idea and sharing it.

I'm using the term *idea* very broadly. It can be a book, a theory, an insight, an improvement. The particular and personal idea that we have may not be original, if there is such a thing as a truly original idea; originality doesn't matter. It may not make us a cent, and it may not curse us with fame; but it will link us with our fellows; it will make us heroes in our own hearts. It will allow us, in Stevenson's phrase, to repay the world's scorn with service; it will allow us to put luster on that nobility that Stevenson rightly says we each and all possess; it will allow us to pursue good, as Stevenson notes that we are driven to do.

My colleague Jon Bragdon here has often remarked to me how each and every one of us should clarify and formulate his or her thinking and write something authentic as an exercise in self-definition, in being human. After the presentation by John Hitchcock in this very room last fall, which several of you attended, Jon told me that he admired Dr. Hitchcock in particular because Dr. Hitchcock knew what his own beliefs were and could articulate them. This is a variation on the comment erroneously attributed to Voltaire: "I disapprove of what you say, but I will defend to the death your right to say it." Jon Bragdon essentially said to me, "I do not agree with all of John Hitchcock's opinions, but I honor him for his eminently human and highly successful effort to communicate those opinions to his fellows."

Clearly we cannot wait upon the convenience of editors on Mars—excuse me, I mean in New York—before we formulate and share those precious ideas. We have to seize the time, not wait for it. I described *Tales of Arcadia* to someone recently, and the next day, after some reflection, she said to me, "I just wanted you to know that I'm glad you got the opportunity to publish your book."

I said, "I appreciate your thought, but I take exception to the way you express it. I didn't 'get an opportunity to publish,' I made the opportunity."

She was a little startled at my answer, and hastily attempted to correct herself by saying: "What I mean is I'm glad you had the chance to publish it."

To which I replied, "I still can't go along with the way you put it. Chance is a matter of luck, and this is one instance where people have to make their own luck."

She was still taken aback; but after a moment's thought she said: "Well, let me just say that I'm glad you published it."

And I replied: "That's something I can't take exception to."

So this is my plea: Make the computation of your life yourself; determine its worth in your own heart. Have an idea—discover what that idea is, whether it is a novel or a work of nonfiction; whether it is a painting or a song; whether it is a baby you have birthed or a house you have built—and find some way to express it, to share it with the rest of us, even if only with the little group in this room.

And be content with that small group that has heard you. If it is difficult to be content with such a limited audience, remember that there is no telling what that small group will do with what you have shared. Swedenborg is just one example of this; he self-published a thousand copies of his magnum opus and in the first year sold how many through his bookseller—one? a few at most? Yet today there are several entire organizations devoted to reprinting his works, and his ideas have spread to every continent.

Furthermore, while I am using Swedenborg as an example, note that he made no attempt to keep his writings alive beyond his own lifetime, trusting to Divine Providence to do that. We focus, foolishly I think, on the afterlife of our ideas. We want them to be in everyone's face forever, and in doing so we overreach ourselves and spoil our own individual heroism. Our part in human history is not to become the great name that all will recognize, but to start a little ripple in the right direction; which, combined with other ripples, will become a wave; which, gaining force, will become a tsunami that will sweep away hate and violence and everything that makes us less than fully human. But the part of any single one of us is necessarily very small.

You all know, I think, that I had a grandmother, very much beloved by all of her ten grandchildren, who taught

Bible for well over fifty years. She wrote a very good guide to the Bible for students, which she self-published and sold out of her own living room and in her classes. That book has been in print for twenty-eight years and has sold something like twelve thousand copies. If we include another book she wrote and a taped version of her course, the sales of her little cottage industry total over two hundred and forty thousand dollars. (Incidentally, she never in all those years showed a profit from her press.)

In 1986, at the age of ninety, she asked me if I would take over running the press when she died. She believed that what she had created was a positive gift to the world, which in fact it was; and she wanted it to continue after her departure. I was in my early thirties then and still under the delusion that I would live forever and would have abundant time to do her work as well as my own. I was touched by her trust and agreed to take over for her when she passed on, which she did in 1990.

On the face of it, her desire to give continuation to the fruit of her life work seems understandable, even praiseworthy. But I have come to see that running her press, continuing her contribution, impedes me in making my own. And I think it was an error in judgment on her part to want her contribution to go on beyond her time. She had started her ripple; she had done the utmost any of us can do. She should not then have prevented me from making mine.

I am not suggesting that we should abandon the works of the past. Sometimes our own "big idea" consists in carrying another's idea from the past into the present in a new form. Whether we are interested in Jung or Bertrand Russell, in Rumi or Yeats, we can make a new idea out of the old and add our own ripple to the wave.

I think as humans we tend to underestimate ourselves and the products of our thought. In part this is merely the neurosis of our species, a permanent inferiority complex we have. "If God did not exist, it would be necessary to invent him," said Voltaire; and perhaps this is true because we have so little affection for ourselves that we foolishly need the vision of something superior to us to give our lives meaning.

Yet as one who believes in the Divine, though not in any form that is effable or that would be recognizable to anyone else, I believe that we as humans are in a sense indistinguishable from the Divine. We are the Divine, and the Divine is us. By becoming more human we become more divine; and by becoming more divine, we become more human. I don't expect this inadequate articulation will make sense to anyone but me; but I think I can communicate the notion that ideas feed us, feed the spirit in us, the better part of us, however you want to define that. Recently a line from Swedenborg leapt into focus for me: "Information, intelligence, and wisdom are spiritual nourishment the way food is natural nourishment." We need to feed the human spirit with ideas, with sound information and with wisdom. In that we can each play our part.

So get busy and publish.

# A Lost Story

# Magenta

> What good does it do you to travel
> a thousand miles, if you find not the
> door into yourself?
>
> —Anonymous

There is a long hill on the road into Stetton; the folk around about call it Horsebane Hill, either because the herb once grew there, or because it is the bane of every horse that climbs it. On one humid day in late spring an old nag was toiling up its long stretch, pulling an even older wagon. The owner had descended to the dust, out of mercy for his beast, though he had second thoughts about his generosity, and glanced from time to time at the seat he had left and at the shade of the patched canvas bonnet that covered the wagon from front to back.

About midway up the hill, horse and driver came up on a woman who was also laboring up the slope. The man was now very heated and a little irritated; and as he drew alongside the woman and looked at her, he seemed to see nothing that would inspire him to civility.

She was badly out of shape. Her dress, of the loudest possible pink, was soaked with perspiration, to which the dust of the road clung in grimy mockery. In her hands she carried two suitcases of enormous size—of so enormous a size, in fact, that she could barely heft them off the ground; and from the way she struggled it appeared that they must have been extremely heavy. Perhaps he thought her disgusting, perhaps ludicrous;

at any rate, he did not speak, but pressed on ahead, slowly gaining a yard or two.

Then he heard a noise and an abrupt exclamation. He turned around. One of the suitcases had broken open. Inside were gowns and other fine clothing, clearly very expensive as well as voluminous. But what struck him—so forcibly that he laughed, hot and exhausted though he was—was that every article in the suitcase was pink.

"My God, dear lady!" he said, in the pompous diction he constantly affected, "I observe you are fond of pink!"

She stood panting, perspiring, almost groaning with discomfort, the tears of her frustration mingling with her sweat. He looked at her more closely and began to pity her for some reason. Clucking to the horse, he set the brake and then approached her.

She made no move to gather up contents of the burst case. He did so for her, stuffing them into the valise once more and lashing the straps tightly, although he showed little concern for the pink material that stuck out on all sides of the leather when he was through.

"Now I have done you that favor," he said, "you owe me one in return. All I ask is that you tell me why you're carrying such an absurd amount of weight with you."

"They're my gowns," she said. "I have to have them."

"Why? Where are you going that you could possibly wear so many? Don't you consider it a good rule never to travel with more luggage than you can easily carry yourself?"

"I want to be stylish," she said bluntly. "I don't feel right if I'm not stylish."

"And in the name of stylishness you'll subject yourself to this torture?"

"It's easy for you to criticize," she snapped. "You have a horse and wagon."

"My dear, absurd creature, my horse and wagon are at your disposal."

"I don't need them!"

"Don't be still more absurd, dear lady."

She glowered at him stubbornly. He took the suitcase he had closed up for her and heaved it into the back of the wagon.

"What are you doing?" she cried.

"If you want to watch over your precious gowns, you'll have to ride. Now don't be foolish. Up! Up onto the seat! You'll ride and I'll walk; if need be, I'll push the wagon. Now—up!"

He took the other valise away from her and hoisted that into the back of the wagon too. She limped to the side and climbed onto the seat with difficulty, yet still with an air of urgency that suggested more that she was afraid her clothing would be stolen than that she felt relief at not having to walk any farther.

Her demeanor changed, however, once she was settled in the shade of the canvas. She gave him a grateful glance. He released the brake, clucked on the horse, and began toiling along beside the wagon again.

"May I ask your name, absurd lady?" he asked, in his usual tone of mock politeness.

"My name is Margaret," she said. "But my hus—but my friends just call me Pinkie."

"Pinkie! What kind of a name is that for a fashionable lady touring the wide world? Hardly a stylish cognomen, my dear. You need a color that suggests more character. Besides, my name is Pinctor. People meeting us might presume more of the relationship

than was proper—Pinkie and Pinctor. May I propose
. . . Magenta?—Some alteration of your wardrobe may
be necessary, of course. But a lady who is willing to
sacrifice all—perhaps even her life—for the sake of
style, would think nothing of casting away all her pink
things and beginning over as Magenta."

She seemed to blush, pinker and hotter under her
heated flush; but she made no attempt to retort.

"And by the way," he said, "if you see anything of
mine in the wagon that can be of use to you, help
yourself to it."

She cast a glance behind her into the interior. Besides
her luggage she saw only a small carpetbag and an even
smaller hard case; the case was strapped to some sort
of portable easel.

It was evident that he followed his own rule about
traveling light. He smiled as he saw her chagrin.

They fared on in silence.

About sunset the axletree broke. They had long since
passed through Stetton Village, where Magenta had
declined to be set down; when Pinctor inquired as to
her ultimate destination, she kept a stubborn silence.
He then guessed she had no goal at all, and teased her
about her aimlessness until her confusion confessed the
truth of his conjecture. He began to tease her again
when the axle snapped.

"It was your suitcases, Magenta," he exclaimed, examining the fractured shaft.

"It was not," she protested desperately, perhaps a
little afraid that he was right.

"Well, now you see why you should never trust to
a conveyance."

"At least we still have the horse," she pointed out.

"Correction: At least I still have the horse."

"Well, we can put the luggage on her, can't we?"

He surveyed the sorry state of the nag and shook his head. "Not tonight," he said. "The poor thing is almost broken."

"So what do we do?"

"We camp here."

"But we have no food," she cried.

"I have a little something. And I'll be willing to share it with you, on condition that you prepare it. Deal?"

"What will you be doing?"

"Observing the sunset. Indulging in painterly transports. What I usually do."

Apparently this kind of silliness did not offend her. "All right," she agreed.

He produced a bag of dried chickpeas, a small sack of herbs, a very small pot, and some matches. From these, before the darkness had quite come over them, Magenta made a good fire and a meal of sorts. She was evidently quite capable, though she huffed a good deal as she went about her work.

"You cook very well for a fine lady," said Pinctor as he ate his supper. His persiflage made her nervous; she could not turn it back on him. "One might almost think— forgive me for saying it—that you were a farmer's wife."

"Maybe I was . . . once," she replied.

"Oh, Magenta! Running away?"

"And what if I am? My husband never notices me. All he thinks about is the farm. If we put this in corn and that in rye; if we get the hay in before it rains; if we scrimp and save; if we could just buy that little corner where the stream runs across—he lives in the future—nothing is ever good enough for him today. He grumbles because the house needs paint; he grumbles because he says the kitchen isn't good enough for me; he grumbles because the lane is washed out and we can't afford to haul more gravel. Do we ever have fun? Do we ever go to a fair together, or spend a few extra pennies on market day? Does he ever buy me a ribbon or a new hat? No—he's living in tomorrow already. Today is already gone by."

"Where did you get your wardrobe, if he's such a scrimper?"

She blushed guiltily. "I took some of the savings," she said. "Why shouldn't I? I worked for that money too."

"You took some of the savings and spent it—on dresses?"

"I did."

"Extraordinary! Did it make you feel better, to do that?"

She nodded determinedly.

He sat back and considered her for some time.

"There's only one flaw in your plan, Magenta," he said.

"What's that?"

"If you stay with your husband, someday all those memories—of deprivation and striving—will all be good. But if you leave him, they'll all be bitter."

"How do you know?"

"I know. Believe me. Besides, I know his disease. I once had it myself. With my painting. Nothing I ever did was good enough. I kept looking for the masterwork, the painting that would establish me as the greatest of all time. I forgot to enjoy my art—to live in each moment of creation. I forgot to thank

God every day I opened my eyes, every time I drew a breath, every time I looked out over this magnificent world."

"And what changed you?"

He laughed, a little startled. "Why, strange to say, Magenta, it was losing a very good woman. She loved me the way I was; she didn't need me to reach the peak of my profession; but I wouldn't accept her love until I had proved to myself that I was the best on earth."

"What did she do?"

"She married someone else. She's almost happy with him, too. I'm sure much happier than she would have been with me, as I used to be."

"Well, my husband will never change. Never."

"What about you? Will you change?"

"Why should I change?"

"Look at you, my dear! Look at those absurd valises! Do you really think you need that finery just to be you? As if lugging around appurtenances could bring you happiness! It's baggage—the baggage of your own self-loathing."

"Self-loathing! What are you talking about?"

"If you loved yourself, would you need all that frippery? Look at me." He gestured at his own clothing as he sprawled by the fire, genuinely at ease with himself and the world, though his trousers and jacket were patched and worn.

"You're not very stylish," she sniffed.

"What's style, but our guess at how others look at us? Why spend your life in guessing at others' judgments? Rely upon your own—provided that your own is a good one."

She hung her head, her pretense of pride instantly forgotten. "Why should I have a good opinion of myself?" she asked. "I'm too fat."

"Your fat, my dear, is not real. You are not fat. You only have that opinion of yourself. It's like your luggage. You carry that opinion about because you don't believe that you're beautiful."

"I *was* beautiful once," she said. "But I didn't know it. I was . . . not so fat then. Not skinny, but not fat either. My husband used to say I was just right."

"And one day," said Pinctor, "you were eating a piece of your own apple pie, and you said, 'I think I'll have another. What does it matter? I'm ugly anyway. My husband doesn't care about me; nobody does. Why shouldn't I enjoy myself?'"

"Why shouldn't I?" she asked defiantly.

"*Are* you enjoying yourself?"

She seemed perplexed at the question. She evidently felt she should be enjoying life, and was at a loss to know why she was not.

"But I can't get rid of this weight," she said. "I've tried."

"I'll teach you how," said Pinctor, licking his spoon carefully before he put it away in his pocket. "Tomorrow, Magenta, I shall teach you how to become yourself again."

Her moonlike face lit with hope; which was soon concealed behind a damp cloud of doubt.

The next morning the horse was lame. Pinctor sold the beast to a passing farmer, along with the wagon. After the farmer had led off the limping nag, Magenta voiced her dismay. "What did you do that for?"

"Now I'm free," said Pinctor, jingling the few coins he had gained in the transaction. "Come along, Magenta. We must search for the right light."

"The right light?"

"You'll see. Pick up your suitcases, my dear.—Unless you've a mind to leave them behind?"

"Never!"

"My, my, you're full of nevers, aren't you? Come along. You've got to keep up with me."

They took their respective luggage out of the broken wagon and set off on foot.

"Where is the right light?" asked Magenta.

"Generally you'll find that it's in the high places."

"Ugh," she said.

They walked for some hours. Pinctor seemed to dart backwards and forwards, exclaiming over this view or that, analyzing the light, exhorting Magenta to keep up. She struggled along in the shortest course from point to point, her suitcases beside her, banging against her knees.

All they had had to eat was a bit of leftover chickpeas. Pinctor bought a loaf of coarse bread and some cheese at a farm they passed; but he would not consider eating it until noon.

When the sun was high they stopped on a stretch of the road where a burned-out farmhouse gave them some protection from the heat. There Pinctor divided the loaf and the cheese. Magenta, almost fainting, wolfed down her share in mingled agony and relief. Then she had nothing to do but watch as he lingered over his meal, savoring every bite.

When he was finished he stood up to move on. "I thought you were going to show me how to get thin today," she said.

"I didn't say that. I said that I would help you *become yourself* again. And that requires something more, something very important."

"What? What is it?"

"Patience! Patience!"

"Ugh! Patience is just a way of saying *never.*"

"Not at all. We gain nothing in life except through patience. Whatever you pray for, Magenta, will be granted—when it's right for you to have it, and in the form that it's right for you to have."

"Don't preach to me, Mr. Pinctor. I can't bear it just now."

"You just sit still, then. We'll both hold our peace. Sit—sit just over there. On that beam—yes, that should do nicely."

She did as she was asked, making no attempt to conceal her relief that they were not to trudge on immediately.

By prowling around the ruins, he found an old weathered board about a foot broad and a foot long, which he set up on his easel. Then he set to work with his paints.

"Are you painting me?" she asked suddenly.

"Who else?"

"In this dirty old rag? Let me put on a fresh gown."

He smiled pityingly. "Very well," he said. "As you wish."

She dragged her cases to a private spot and soon returned clad in a gown of searing pink.

"Do you like the color?" she asked as she sat again.

He seemed almost to wince. "It defies my palette," he said.

"But do you like it?"

"Well, let's just say it's not to my palate."

And chuckling at his pun, he set to work.

He did not hold his peace as he had promised. He spoke of almost everything, and almost nothing. He chattered about colors and light, he teased her to stay awake, he told stories of his wandering days. Nor did he sit still. He strutted close to her, backed away, and wandered about the ruins, although he would not allow her to change her posture.

And gradually there emerged on the dry, gray wood a picture of Magenta. But not the Magenta that was here, now, propped on a timber in her straining pink gown. Instead this was another Magenta: the Magenta as she once had been, within the gaudy and distracting finery. Her face in the picture was not round, though it was healthy and full; he seemed to have found the cheeks and jawbones, extracted the structure of the nose and forehead from beneath its concealing weight. He depicted her in a simple white dress. Her chest within it was full, but not matronly; she had a waist again, though it was not that of a girl. The woman in the portrait was a beautiful Magenta, or at least a handsome one.

The sun was declining when he stood up and began packing away his paints.

"Can I look now?" she asked eagerly.

"Of course."

She waddled hastily over to his side and stared at the painting.

For a minute she was silent with astonishment. Then she almost shouted aloud.

"It's me!" she said.

He laughed heartily. "Now that," he said, "I shall consider among the rarest compliments I have ever received. 'It's me!' she says. Of course it's you, you silly creature!"

"But I mean *me*, the old me—the way I used to be."

"Correction, Magenta—the way you are now."

He paused and waited for her full attention. "This, my dear," he said, "is the true Magenta. The Magenta you should love and be proud of.'"

There was a kind of hope in her eyes now.

"Can I have it?" she asked. "Can I have the picture?"

"Of course you can. It's yours. I want you to look at it every day. I want you to look at it so often that it becomes a part of you. So that if this painting is ever lost or destroyed, you will still see it in your mind— until the day comes that you see it in your mirror."

She stared at the painting again, as if awed by its power.

"And the dress is so pretty, too," she said. "I never thought white could look so pretty. Even my wedding dress was pink."

He grimaced and then finished packing his things. "You'll have to find some way to carry it, though," he said. "I won't carry it for you."

"I'll put it in my valise."

"I don't think so—the paint will smear, you know. It will take months to dry, really."

"I know what I'll do. I have a hatbox in one case—it's full of stockings. I'll—I'll throw away the stockings and put the picture in that. Will that work?"

"Properly packed and braced, it might do," he said. He looked at her with a rueful smile. "And it is a beginning, I guess," he added.

She hurried to make the adjustment to her luggage. As she worked he watched her, considering.

"I take it you have no money, Magenta?" he asked after a long silence.

"No," she confessed.

"Spent it all on gowns?"

"Uh huh."

"Very well. I shall hire you then. You shall be cook. I'll supply food for us both; you'll prepare it. Deal?"

"Yes, sir," she said.

"Good, then. Let's away. We've a walk before supper."

Magenta found, as the spring passed away, and the summer came on, that she had to walk for her supper every day. Sometimes they stopped at a fair so that Pinctor could paint and peddle his pictures; sometimes in the precinct of a little village he would set up studio and paint deacons and deacons' wives; and when he was particularly low on cash, he would paint some farmer's family for a good dinner. He was perpetually in his last few coins; and yet not once did Magenta lie down to sleep at the end of a day with an empty stomach.

During the days, though, was a different matter. They made a strange couple: the thin man in his ragged clothing, frisking ahead or behind, enthusing about the views or the changing perspectives of the hills; the fat woman in her gay dresses, staggering along with her great valises, groaning about her hunger and her weariness. They became known; word went ahead of them, and they found they were expected when they came into the sleepy little villages of the hills. People knew they were neither married nor lovers; just an odd pair life had cast together for a time.

And the hard life was not without its effect. One day Magenta noticed that her favorite gown looked baggy on her. Gradually her arms hardened; instead of shivering flab they became smooth, taut muscle; and she carried the suitcases, if not with ease, at least with control. She found the hills easier; she found she sweated less; she found, curiously enough, that she grew less hungry as she regained her natural size.

One day in August—it was particularly hot—they were working their way up the switchbacks in a high notch in the Gray Mountains. They came around a bend that gave out on a precipitous drop of perhaps a thousand feet. In the valley below, by a distant river, herds of miniscule cattle dotted the tawny grass; a miniature hamlet seemed a bundle of brown mush-rooms sprung out of a patch of moss. For a minute they stared, breathing hard.

"I must!" cried Pinctor finally.

By now she knew what he meant. She sat down on her suitcases while he set up his easel and began painting on a dirty canvas he had stretched over a crude frame. He hummed and bustled in his characteristic manner.

After a quarter hour he stopped suddenly and looked at Magenta. "You seem very quiet, my dear," he said. (By now his familiarity had lost most of its irony and become a simple habit.)

In fact she was not any more quiet than usual; but he had correctly sensed that her thoughts were more serious than usual, and would soon result in action.

Very abruptly she stood up. "God!" she cried. "I've had enough!"

She kicked over one of her suitcases and tore at the binding frantically, as if afraid she would change her mind before she could act. Pinctor looked at her first in amazement, and then in slowly dawning comprehension and delight. He set aside his palette and brush, rubbed his hands together, and turned fully about to watch.

She wrenched the case open and plunged her fingers into the pink innards of her vanity. "Yes!" she cried, in a frenzy. "I'll do it! I'll do it!" She drew out the contents indiscriminately, wadded them into a ball, lofted them over her head, and staggered perilously close to the brink of the cliff. Pinctor started as if to catch her, but relaxed as she caught herself.

"Good riddance!" she shouted, hurling the ball of finery out into space.

"Good job, Magenta!" exclaimed Pinctor.

She looked around, as if she had forgotten his presence. He realized he had broken upon her frenzy.

"Now the other," he said.

"No," she said, in an altered voice.

"Why didn't I keep my mouth shut?" he muttered.

She went back to the suitcase and looked confusedly at its emptiness, as if she had already forgotten her own actions.

"Another day," he said.

"What?"

"I said, another day. There's time enough for everything."

He went back to his painting. Magenta, after staring stupidly at the suitcases for some time, knelt down and began to divide the contents of the one valise between the two.

By September they found themselves wending back over much of the ground they had traveled already.

Pinctor began to talk about the light in winter, as if that season were already upon them. Magenta had only one dress warm enough for the cool mornings and afternoons. She had to take it in at every seam before she could wear it.

One day they stopped in a village on the high road that led down out of the hill country. Pinctor led the way into a busy inn and ordered food in abundance: mountain trout, a good ham, a half dozen tarts, dark ale and creamy milk. But when it came, neither of them ate more than a few bites.

"Not hungry, I see, Magenta," he observed.

"I could eat," she said indifferently. "I just don't want to."

"Ah!"

"What about you? You usually enjoy your food. You enjoy everything."

"Today, Magenta, my dear, is a day, I confess, that I am not enjoying."

"I noticed you seemed a little out of sorts. Why is that?"

"Because some time in the next hour or so the coach comes down the road, and I must be on it."

"The coach? You mean we're going to ride? What for?"

He shook his head. "Magenta, you have always been so careless of pronouns. Ever since that first day. I've let them go by, all this time, without correction; but this time I really must . . . I said 'I,' 'I,' Magenta, not 'we.'"

"Oh," she said.

The silence, amid the clatter of the inn, was long between them.

"I must go back, you see. To the city. I've things to do. There are faces there I must paint, in the winter, just as here among the hills I must paint the face of nature in the summer."

"But you haven't kept your paintings. You've given them all away—sold them—lost them—"

"No, no, my dear. I have them all—in here," he said, tapping his heart. "The golden hours—all here."

She looked a little scared, a little hurt; and yet only a little.

"What about—" she began.

"What about you? Yes, what about you, Magenta? I've thought about that. And I've decided, Magenta, that you don't need me anymore."

"I was going to say, 'What about the picture you gave me?'"

"Oh!" he said. Then he smiled. "That! Yes, that one. That one, that one too is in my heart, Magenta."

They sat without saying anything more for a long time. The serving maid came and he paid her. Still they sat.

Finally, from far down the high road, came the sound of the coach. Pinctor stood, fussily plucking at his scant luggage.

"Will you come say goodbye to me?" he asked.

"No," she said. "I won't say goodbye to you. Because you're in my heart, too, Mr. Pinctor. I'll never forget you. You gave me back my self."

"Not at all," he said. "You took it back."

"Well," she said, "I'll come out and wish you a pleasant journey."

"I would be pleased! Pleased indeed!"

She followed him out of the inn onto the edge of the roadway. The next few minutes were all a bustling and shouting, men and boys running here and there, dogs barking, passengers descending and ascending from the coach, luggage being stowed and lashed. In the midst of the din Pinctor turned to her and thrust a knotted handkerchief into her hands.

"Here," he said.

"What is it?"

"A few coins. To see you on your way."

She put the kerchief in a pocket and pressed her fingertips to her eyes suddenly.

He was the last to climb on the step. The coachman was gathering his whip to crack it over the heads of the horses. The painter looked back at Magenta, who lifted her face to him bravely.

"One last thing, Magenta," he said.

"What's that?"

"Have you seen yourself in a mirror lately?"

She smiled.

"I don't need a mirror," she said. "I have your picture, remember?"

He laughed. The whip cracked; the horses sprang away; and that was the last she saw of him, laughing, blowing a kiss, waving cheerily.

When she turned around, she discovered that her suitcases had by accident been loaded on the coach.

That harvest time, on a farm some way south of Farr, a man was cutting wheat with his neighbors and hired hands. It was hard work, and the whole crew of men, women, and children had been hard at it for ten days now, moving from one farm to the next. As this was his own place, the man was very anxious that the job be done right, that the weather not turn bad, that his helpers be given the best food and the best refreshment he had to offer, and that he work harder than any of them. The long line of mowers was working up through the golden wheat in unison; and though the day was new, and the work but just begun, he had hope that all would go well.

And so it did; it went on well until sometime in midmorning. At that point he looked up the line and saw someone he had not noticed earlier. "Josh," he said to the man next to him, "who's that woman in the white dress at the far end of the line? Is it that cousin of Hammond's as he said was coming to help?"

"I reckon," said Josh. "Swings a mean scythe, doesn't she? We'll have to sharpen when we get acrost; ask Hammond then."

They went back to their mowing; but the farmer could not leave the wondering alone. Often he twisted in his stroke to look over his shoulder at the strong, capable figure scything the wheat with a brisk, bold swing of her arms and torso.

Then, when they had a quarter of the field left to cross, suddenly the man flung down his scythe and stared at the woman. His work forgotten, he turned toward her and began walking, almost stalking, across the broad field. He seemed dazed; the mowers stopped, one by one, as they sensed something wrong with him; all except the last mower, she in white.

He stood beside her, but still she did not stop.

"God be praised!" he cried, weeping.

Then she stayed her hand. Her cheek was flushed. She leaned on the handle of the scythe and pushed her hair as if to set it out of her face. She looked at the horizon, not at the man, though she was all conscious of him.

"Yes," she said, "God be praised."

"Have you come back, then?"

"If you'll have me."

"Have you? If you'll have me, you mean! I've changed my ways. I call on God to witness I have. I won't be so hard driven, lass."

She smiled, looking out over the field. "Oh, won't you, now?" she said. Her tone was a little like that of Pinctor, teasing; as if she knew her husband too well to expect much, but was pleased with the intention.

"Look at you!" he said. "You look like the bride I brought home! What's happened to you?"

She finally faced him. "I'm back," she said. "I've been gone a long while. Longer even than you know. But now I'm back."

He strode close to her, but paused, as if almost afraid of her beauty.

"Say you'll stay, Pinkie!"

"No, I'll not stay Pinkie. I'm sick of pink. I want you to call me by another name. I'll stay by that."

"What shall I call you, then?"

She hesitated a moment.

"Maggie," she said. "I want you to call me Maggie."

www.ingramcontent.com/pod-product-compliance
Lightning Source LLC
Chambersburg PA
CBHW061540210726

48287CB00006B/2027